Fredric Brown was born in Cincinnati, Ohio, and attended the University of Cincinnati and Hanover College in Indiana but never received a degree. He worked in an office from 1924 to 1936, when he left to become a proofreader and writer for the *Milwaukee Journal*. He also began writing fiction and in 1936 sold the first of more than three hundred published short stories. Because of a chronic respiratory condition, he left the Midwest to live in Taos, New Mexico, and then Tucson, Arizona. He lived briefly in Los Angeles, too, writing scripts for Alfred Hitchcock's television programs. In addition to his mysteries, Mr. Brown wrote numerous science fiction stories and novels, including *What Mad Universe* and *Martians Go Home*.

Otto Penzler, series editor of Quill Mysterious Classics, owns The Mysterious Bookshop in New York City. He is the publisher of The Mysterious Press and *The Armchair Detective* magazine. Mr. Penzler co-authored, with Chris Steinbrunner, the *Encyclopedia of Mystery and Detection*, for which he received the Edgar Allan Poe Award from the Mystery Writers of America.

THE
DEEP END

THE
DEEP END

FREDRIC BROWN

A Quill Mysterious Classic

Series Editor:
OTTO PENZLER

Quill
New York

Library of Congress Catalog Card Number: 84-60846

ISBN: 0-688-03919-7

Printed in the United States of America

First Quill Edition

1 2 3 4 5 6 7 8 9 10

SATURDAY

· 1 ·

The *Herald* city room was hot enough to bake a cake, although it was only half past ten by the big electric clock on the wall. Half past ten of a Saturday morning in July, the last day before a week's vacation for me.

Up near the ceiling somewhere a fly was making a hell of a commotion. Its buzz sounded louder to me than the sporadic hammer of typewriters. I looked up and located it, a big horsefly going nowhere fast, in circles.

Looking up made my collar tight and I loosened it. You damn fool horsefly, I thought, don't you know there aren't any horses in a newspaper office?

I found myself wondering whether a horsefly starved to death if it didn't find a horse, like the bread-and-butter-fly in *Through the Looking-Glass* that starved to death unless it could find weak tea with cream in it.

Someone standing by my desk said, "What the hell are you doing?"

It was Harry Rowland. I grinned at him. I said, "I was communing with a horsefly. Any objections?"

"Thank God," he said. "I thought you were praying. Ed wants to see you, Sam. Right away." He moved on toward the door. He wore a light tan Palm Beach suit and the back of the coat was soaked through with sweat over the shoulder blades.

I sat there a few more seconds getting up the courage to stand and walk. I'd been getting by without doing anything for almost half an hour and I'd begun to hope that Ed had forgotten me.

Ed is the *Herald's* city editor. A lot of editors are named Ed. It doesn't mean anything. I've known reporters named Frank and Ernest and once I knew a girl named Virginia.

I pushed my way through the stifling air into Ed's office. I sat down in the chair in front of his desk and waited for him to look up, hoping that he wouldn't. But he did.

He said, "Kid just killed on the roller coaster at Whitewater Beach. I want a human interest story, what a swell kid he was, bereaved parents, that kind of stuff. Lay it on thick. You know what I mean."

I knew what he meant. "I'm sobbing already," I told him. "Has the kid got a name?"

"Probably. Get the dope from Rowland."

"He just left."

"On his way out there. He'll write the news story, Sam. And Burgoyne will write an editorial. You—"

"I know," I said. "The sob story. But I've got to have *something* to work on, Ed, unless you want me to wait till Rowland gets back."

"He'll phone you the minute he gets the kid's name and a fact or two to start from. Stick by your phone till he calls. Don't start on anything else. When you hear from him get going and stay with it, clear till deadline if you can get enough dope. Use all the space you can fill. A pic if you can dig one. Hit it hard."

"And make 'em cry," I said.

He shook with silent laughter.

I went back to my desk and sat there waiting for the phone to ring.

Ed hadn't needed to draw me a diagram. I'd worked for the *Herald* eight years, so I knew the score. This was strictly a must job for dear old Yale. I'd known that the minute he mentioned Whitewater Beach, which is the amusement resort just outside of town. The *Herald* didn't carry Whitewater Beach advertising and the *Herald* never mentioned Whitewater Beach unless someone was injured or robbed there, and then we really went to town. This was the first time anyone had ever been *killed* there and the sky was going to be the limit.

You see, Whitewater Beach was owned by a man named Walter A. Campbell who topped our s. o. b. list. Colonel Ackerman, owner of the *Herald*, hated Campbell's guts with an abiding hatred. The feud between them went back over a dozen years. The most common version of how it had started was that Campbell had called the Colonel a crooked politician because Ackerman, then heading the city council, had blocked a paving project that would have improved the main route to Whitewater Beach; Campbell accused Ackerman of doing it for purposes of extortion, to force the amusement park to advertise more heavily in the *Herald*.

So now, because Colonel Ackerman never forgot or forgave an insult, I sat waiting for my phone to ring, like a runner waiting for the starter's gun. But waiting was all right with me; I didn't want to work anyway. I hoped the phone would never ring. So, of course, it rang.

But when I said, "Sam Evans," into it, it wasn't Rowland's voice that answered; it was Millie's.

"I thought I'd better call to say good-by, Sam," she said. "I'm going to take an earlier train than the one I figured on. I found out there was one at four o'clock this afternoon and that'll be better than the eight-thirty-tonight one because it will get me there late this evening instead of the middle of the night."

I said, "That's fine, Millie, but I'm sorry I won't get a chance to see you again. I thought—well, I hoped we'd have a chance for one more talk before you left. Listen, would you have time to come downtown and have lunch with me?"

"Thanks, but I'd better not. On account of leaving

sooner than I'd planned to I've got an awful lot of things to do. I've hardly started my packing. Good-by, Sam.''

"Wait," I said. "You won't have to leave more than half an hour before train time. I'll see if I can get off at two o'clock as soon as the final goes in. Then I can get home in time to help you with a few things and we can talk a little, and then I can drive you to the station so you won't have to take a taxi.''

"Thanks, Sam, but—please don't. I don't think we *should* talk any more, not until we've each been away for a week and have had time to think things over by ourselves. We've each said everything there is to say until then.''

"Maybe, but—''

"Have a good time on your hunting trip, Sam. Good-by.''

"Good-by, Millie," I said.

And the phone clicked in my ear before I could put it down. The click seemed to have an oddly final sound.

I put down the phone and sat staring at it, feeling a little empty inside, wondering how final that click had been. Was it going to be the end of things between us? Oh, we'd see one another again after our respective trips. But would we ever be *together* again, or would it be just to compare notes and agree to disagree on a permanent basis? Would it be to discuss at last the ugly seven-letter word neither of us had actually mentioned yet, the seven-letter word which would mean the end of almost five years of marriage?

It was to think that over, each of us apart from the other, that we'd arranged separate vacations. I was going hunting and fishing with two friends of mine, one of whom owned a little summer cabin on a lake fifty miles north of the city; Millie was going to spend the week with her sister and brother-in-law in Rockford. She might stay longer than the week if she decided to, but one week was all the vacation I still had coming; I'd taken a week in advance early in the spring when my brother in Cincinnati had undergone a dangerous operation and I'd wanted to be with him.

That week had come out all right; he'd pulled through nicely. But how would this coming week turn out? Would our marriage pull through?

I didn't want to think about it just then. And suddenly I wanted something to do besides just sit and wait for the phone to ring.

It occurred to me that maybe I could get myself something to start on before Rowland's call came. I picked up my phone and asked the switchboard girl for the South Side Police Station. A moment later I recognized Louie Brandon's voice answering. I asked him if he had anything yet on a kid killed at Whitewater.

"Just a quick report. Kid's name was—just a minute—Henry O. Westphal, six-oh-three Irving Street, age seventeen. Father is Armin Westphal, owns a hosiery and lingerie store downtown."

I had that on copy paper by the time he finished. I asked, "Where's the body? Still there?"

"They're taking it to Haley's. That's the undertaking parlor nearest to Whitewater Beach. The address is nineteen hundred South—"

"I know where it is," I said. "Who made identification?"

"Wallet in his pocket. We're trying to get in touch with his parents. They're out of town for the day and we haven't reached them yet."

"Heard he was killed on the Blue Streak. Fall out of a car?"

"No. Got run over by one, climbing across the tracks."

"Okay, Louie. Thanks."

I had something to start on now. Since the father, Armin Westphal, was a businessman there'd probably be a clipping or two on him in our morgue that would give me some background.

I called the morgue. "Got anything on an Armin Westphal?"

"Just a minute."

I sat and waited, staring up at the ceiling again. The horsefly was still flying around up there looking for a horse.

•2•

The telephone said, "There's an envelope, yes."

"Good. There isn't by any chance anything on a Henry Westphal, is there? Henry O. Westphal?"

"Why didn't you ask for both at once and save me a trip? Wait a minute."

I waited a minute.

"Yes, there's an envelope on him too."

"I'll be damned," I said. "I'll send down for both envelopes."

I caught a copy boy and sent him. He was back in a few minutes and put two nine-by-twelve manila envelopes on my desk. I picked up Armin Westphal's first to get it out of the way.

There were four clippings in it. One of them was a real break, a biographical sketch with a picture. A few years before we'd run a series of brief biographies of local merchants—chosen, needless to say, by the advertising department and run on the business page. Armin Westphal had made the grade and I had more dope on him than I could possibly use. The picture, just a half-column head, looked familiar; I'd seen him somewhere. A dour-looking man whom you'd never guess to be a purveyor of hosiery and lingerie. The cut for that picture would still be in the cut racks up in the composing room and it was one we could use effectively. The dour expression made it fit; you don't like to run a cheerful or smiling picture of a man whom you're describing as a grief-stricken father. The other three clippings were short ones and more recent. They concerned Chamber of Commerce activities and gave me the clue as to where I'd seen him; several years ago I'd covered a couple of Chamber of Commerce banquets and he'd spoken at one of them, very boringly.

I opened the Henry O. Westphal envelope. There were two pictures in it, both glossy prints taken by *Herald* staff photographers.

One was a football shot, the kid in uniform and helmet, poised for a drop-kick. Except that he looked big and husky for seventeen—or more likely sixteen since the shot had been taken last fall and it was now July—you couldn't tell much about him. Not even his build, for sure; he might have been tall and thin and the rest of it padding.

The other shot was much better; it was waist-up and was a picture of a grinning, good-looking kid in a white sweat-shirt holding a tennis racket. The date stamped on the back showed it had been taken only six weeks ago. It had been blocked down in crayon for a halftone but apparently the cut hadn't been made or the glossy wouldn't be in the file envelope. A cut would be made of it now, all right, probably a two-column one.

There were five or six clippings. The most recent one, the top one, was only five weeks old. It was about Westphal's performance in the state high school tennis tournament. He'd gone there representing South Side High—my own alma mater, as it happened—and, after being seeded eighteenth, had placed fourth in the tournament. Each of the other high schools in town had sent a player but none of the others had placed near the top. This was the story the picture had been taken for—before he'd left for the capital to play—but the picture hadn't been used.

The other stories were all about football. He'd been

pretty good at it. The oldest clipping was three years old
and got him off to a flying start; as quarterback of the
freshman team he'd led them into a 7-7 tie with the
regular team in that year's intramural game. According
to the other clippings he'd come right along, although
he'd done nothing very spectacular in his sophomore year
except to end that year as first-string halfback—having
switched or having been switched by the coach to that
position. But last fall, as a junior, he'd been South Side's
best player—at least he'd gained more yardage than any
other player. Good as a broken field runner and pass
receiver in particular.

Plenty of material, at least as far as his sports activities
went. Good stuff, too. I could bill him as a would-have-
been star in two sports.

I could wax lyrical about what he would have become
if only he'd stayed away from that place of danger,
Whitewater Beach. I'd damn well *better* wax lyrical if
I wanted to turn out the story that was expected of me.
This made it easy, although probably one of the boys
from the sports department could do a better job of it.
Personally I've never seen why people get interested in,
let alone excited about, spectator sports. Golf, yes. A
bit of hunting or fishing a few times a year. And I play
poker as often as I possibly can without getting Millie
too annoyed at me.

But maybe I wouldn't have that to worry about any
longer. Maybe I'd be able to play poker as often as I
liked—or be driven by loneliness into playing it even
oftener than I liked. Unless, of course, someday—

I pulled my mind away from my personal problems
and back to the story by looking at the picture of the
Westphal kid again. Maybe, if I concentrated on the
cheerful grin he was wearing in that picture, I could work
myself into the proper state of mind to write a really
good tear-jerker.

He *was* a good-looking kid. And the shoulders in that

football picture hadn't been all padding, either. Even in a sweat-shirt he looked plenty husky.

I decided to keep studying the clippings until I got my call from Rowland and picked them up to read them more thoroughly; I'd just skimmed the first time.

I picked up a few things I'd missed. The kid had a nickname, Obie. Probably from his middle name, since the initial was an O. Obadiah, possibly. Somehow, Obie Westphal sounded better than Henry Westphal. Maybe I'd use it that way after the lead; it would give the story an informal touch.

·3·

The phone rang. It was Rowland. He said, "Got paper and pencil ready?"

"Sure. But I've got some of it already, Harry. Called the South Side Police Station and Louie was on the desk and gave me what he had. And I found morgue envelopes on the kid and his father. Here's what I've got so far." And I told him.

"Good," he said. "I can't add much. Get one thing first; we can imply Whitewater was somehow to blame but we can't say so. They weren't. The kid was where he had no business being and he was crossing the tracks right past a danger sign. At the bottom of the first dip; the tracks come down to within a foot of the ground there. Maybe there should have been a railing—that's our only angle—but then again it's around behind concession booths in territory where the public isn't allowed. He had to climb a fence to get back there."

"Anybody see it happen?"

"No. And the car that ran over him was empty—which

was damn lucky. It was derailed and if there'd been any passengers they'd have been injured pretty badly at least. But it was a test run.''

''That something unusual?''

''Hell, no. They do it every day before they open up for business. I guess all roller coasters do. The Blue Streak has two cars and they give each one of them a dry run around the tracks every day before they open. Usually that's early afternoon, but on Saturdays and Sundays in good weather they open in the morning. This happened at a quarter after ten as near as I can get the time.''

''Was the kid pretty mangled?''

''From the chest down, yes. But his head and arms were across the track. They won't have to use a closed coffin.''

''Anything new on the parents being located?''

''No, I guess there's no way they can be reached until they get back, and that won't be until after deadline so we won't have any statement from them for today's paper. Hey, wait a minute—Haley's trying to tell me something.''

I waited a minute and he came back on the wire. ''Haley tells me the parents *have* been reached. They were at Williamsburg, at Mr. Westphal's sister's. They're starting back right away—but it's about a four, maybe five hour drive from there so you still won't have a statement in time.''

''They didn't say anything over the phone, either of them?''

''Not except that they were starting back right away and would come direct to the funeral parlor here. Anything else I can give you, Sam?''

I said, ''I've got plenty on the kid's athletic record, but not much about him outside of that. Have you got a lead on anybody who knew him personally that I could get in touch with?''

"Yes, there is. Right here. Haley's got a high school girl helping out in the office this summer, a vacation job. She knew Westphal, was in some of the same classes with him. I've already talked to her but maybe you'd better get it direct. I can put her on for you."

"Swell, but first what's her name? And can she hear you now?"

"Grace Smith. No, she's in another office; she can't hear me. But listen, be careful what you say to her, will you? This hit her pretty hard; she's been crying and she's still pale around the gills. Try not to set her off again."

"Okay. Was she the kid's sweetheart?"

"I don't think so, but I'd guess she had a crush on him. Bobby-soxer stuff. Well, I guess it's more healthy for 'em to swoon over a high school hero their own age than over some crooner old enough to be their father."

"All right," I said. "Put her on."

About a minute later a girl's voice said, "Hello. This is Grace Smith." She'd been crying hard, all right; I could tell from her voice. It sounded as though it was walking a tightrope and trying not to fall off.

I said, "This is Evans of the *Herald*, Miss Smith. I'm writing an article on Obie Westphal. Not about the accident, just about Obie himself. I'll appreciate anything you can tell me about him."

"He was—he was tops. The best football player in the school, and good at tennis too, really good."

"I've got plenty on his athletic record—but not much else. Can you tell me what kind of student he was? How he did in his classes?"

"Oh, he was smart. He got good grades in everything."

"Was he popular with his classmates? Outside of athletics, I mean?"

"Oh, yes. Everybody was just crazy about him. It's just—just awful that—"

Her voice was wavering on the tightrope and I cut in quickly with a question to distract her. "What course was he taking, Miss Smith? And do you know what he intended to be?''

''The science course. He wasn't sure, but he thought he might decide to be a d-doctor. I was in his English class last year, English Three, and in his Latin class the year before. I think he wanted to be a—you know, a laboratory doctor. The kind that does experiments and learns new things.''

''I see. Do you happen to know how he got the nickname Obie?''

''From his middle name. It's Obadiah. Henry Obadiah Westphal. But nobody ever called him Henry, even the teachers. He even signed his papers Obie.''

''Do you happen to know his family, Miss Smith?''

''I met his father and mother once, at a school party. But I just met them; I don't really know them. His father owns a store, I think; I don't know what kind of store.''

''Any brothers or sisters?''

''N-no. Not that I know of. I'm pretty sure he hasn't—hadn't.''

''Did you know him pretty well personally? Did you have dates with him?''

''N-not exactly. But I've danced with him at dances at the school. S-six times.''

The poor kid, I thought. She had it bad, to have counted those dances like pearls, to have known that it wasn't five times or seven that she'd been that near him. Under other circumstances it could have been funny. It didn't strike me as funny now.

I thought of an angle. If he'd had a regular sweetheart, a steady girl, and if I could reach her by phone I might get some good sob stuff for the story. Maybe he'd even been engaged; there are plenty of puppy-love engagements in the last year or two of high school. I'd been engaged myself in my senior year—to a girl I hadn't seen in six years now, Nina Carberry. I'd heard, though, that she was working in the office at South Side High.

"Did Obie have a steady girl friend, Miss Smith?" I asked.

"No, he didn't. He—he didn't date girls very much. He mostly came stag to school parties and dances, not always but mostly."

I said, "Thanks a lot, Miss Smith. Will you put Rowland back on? If he's still there, that is."

"Yes, he's still here. Just a sec."

When Rowland came back on I said, "Guess I got enough to do it, Harry. But keep me posted if you get anything new. Particularly if you get names of any close friends of the kid, anybody else I can call. Say, he wouldn't have any relatives living in town outside of his parents, would he?"

"Nope. Anyway none of Westphal's employees at his store know of any relatives here. And they probably would. That's how the cops found out the Westphals were visiting Mr. Westphal's sister in Williamsburg. Say, you could get a statement from her by calling long distance, if you got to have a statement from somebody."

"I'll try," I said. "Thanks for the suggestion. Hey, do you know her name?"

"Just a minute; I can get it."

He came back to the phone in a minute and gave me a name and a Williamsburg address; the name was Hattie Westphal, which would make her a maiden aunt of Obie's. And a statement from her would be the next best thing to a statement from one of the parents, and that wouldn't be available, at least not in time for the city edition.

I put in the long distance call and while I was waiting for the connection I cradled the phone between my shoulder and my ear and ran paper into the machine. But before I figured out my lead sentence the operator said, "That number does not answer, sir. Shall I keep trying?"

I told her to keep trying.

But it probably would be useless; if the aunt wasn't

home now it was more than likely that she was returning with the parents in their car.

But damn it, I ought to have a statement from somebody about how wonderful a boy Obie had been, somebody closer to him than Grace Smith had been, somebody whose name— The principal of the high school, of course. It took me a few seconds to remember his name and then I had it. Emerson, Paul E. Emerson. And I was fairly sure he was still principal there. I looked up his home phone number—even if there were summer classes at the school, he wouldn't be there on Saturday—and dialed it. The phone rang but nobody answered it.

I thought again of Nina Carberry. Working in the office of South Side High it was just possible that she could tell me where Emerson could be reached. If not, she could at least give me a fact or two about Obie, maybe the names of some of his teachers who could be reached. I looked up Nina Carberry's number and called it. Again no answer. Some days are like that, nobody home anywhere you call.

I'd have to write the first story without statements, but maybe that was all to the good; some suitable quotes would add up to a good peg on which to hang a follow-up story. And the *Herald* would follow this one up as far as it could be followed. Anyway, I had plenty of material, even without quotes.

Sob story or no, the lead would have to bring in Whitewater Beach. I started typing. I wrote. *Today under the wheels of a Whitewater Beach roller coaster . . .*

It went easy from there and I wrote almost as fast as I could type, but I wrote well. While you're writing a story, you can tell, maybe by the feel of the typewriter keys, whether it's good or not. This one was good. It had what a story took. I forgot while I was writing it that a man named Campbell who owned an amusement park was on the *Herald's* s. o. b. list. I thought about a kid named Obie and I wrote it straight and the tears were there. Maybe *I* wasn't crying, but my tongue wasn't in my cheek either.

I finished it, six pages triple-spaced, with time to spare, so I decided it might as well be accurate too. I'd carried the dates and the home and store addresses in my head and I might as well check them against the file clips. I'd almost finished doing that when the phone rang.

It was Ed. He said, "Kill that story."

By the time it had registered the phone was dead. I put it down and stared at it a few seconds and then I got up and went into Ed's office.

When he looked up I asked him, "What the hell?"

His voice was as sour as the expression on his face. "Rowland just phoned. It wasn't the Westphal kid. It was a light-fingered juvenile delinquent from the Third Ward, with a detention home record a yard long. He'd pinched the other kid's leather; that's how the identification was wrong."

"Swell," I said. "I'd just finished the story. Now do I start one about the poor little pickpocket?"

He glared at me. "Hell no. We can't run a sob on him; we'll have to stick to the news story and an editorial and the less said about the kid himself the better."

"*Nil nisi bonum,*" I said. "Speak only good of the dead. If no bonum, skipum."

He looked even more pained. I didn't blame him. He said, "This is your last day before vacation, isn't it?"

"Uh-huh."

"Go out for lunch now and make it short, half an hour, and then get the hell out of here as soon as the home edition's in at two."

I said, "Thanks," and meant it. The last few hours before a vacation go slowly.

He handed me some sheets of paper. "Here's upstate stuff that came in late; the desk won't have time to handle it. Put it in English as soon as you're back from lunch. Now scram."

I scrammed. I got my suit coat off the back of the chair of my desk and I picked up the Obie Westphal story and made a pass at the wastebasket with it. But I didn't let go. It had been a good story; I wanted to read it over once sometime before I threw it away. I dropped it into a drawer of my desk and closed the drawer so a copyboy wouldn't get hold of it by mistake and take it to the composing room.

Then I went down for a beer and a sandwich at Murphy's, the bar across the street from the *Herald*, and I forgot all about Obie. I thought about the trip I was going to take with Bill and Harvey Whelan and the good time I ought to have if I could forget about the trouble with Millie. And then I found myself thinking again about Nina Carberry, whom I hadn't thought about for years until this morning. Wondering whether, if Millie and I did split up, it might not be interesting to look up Nina sometime and see what six years had done to her, what she was like now. Nina and I had had a very important first experience together when we were in our last year of high school at South Side. But that had been a long time ago and we'd drifted apart during the first year or two after we were out of school. There'd been an argument over something that seemed ridiculous now but we'd each been too proud to give in, and then we'd each found other interests elsewhere. At least I had.

I went back to the *Herald* and to my desk. I started putting the upstate copy into English and sending it, a sheet or two at a time, to the composing room.

Harry Rowland came in and I waved him over to my desk. He sat down on a corner of it.

"Wha' hoppen?" I asked him. "Ed told me it was a different kid, but I didn't ask him how they corrected the identification. Somebody who knew the Westphal kid take a look or what?"

"Fingerprints. They'd taken them for routine, like they do on all D. O. A. cases, and they put 'em through the routine way in spite of the wallet. And the Bureau of Identification digested them and came up with the fact that the prints were on record and they belonged to a Polack kid named Chojnacki. Who's spent most of the last couple of years, since he was fifteen, in reform school and the detention home. Which shows there's maybe something in this routine business. It's tough, though, that they'd already phoned the Westphals that their son was dead.''

"They don't know otherwise yet?''

"No way they can be reached. They won't know until they get back, and that won't be before late afternoon. You know, I think Ed's missing a bet.''

"What?''

"He's running the wrong story. The big human interest angle is the Westphals driving back from Williamsburg thinking their son is dead and how they're going to feel when they find out he isn't. I asked him if I should write that up as a separate story, at least a box item in the main story, and he said no.''

"Why not?''

Rowland grimaced. "Couldn't write it without explaining why the first identification was wrong, why the cops thought it was the Westphal kid. That'd have to bring out the pickpocket angle and he doesn't want that used. Nothing that will detract from the slaps we're taking at Whitewater. And *dear reader* would feel less sympathy for Jimmy Chojnacki if they knew why he was back there behind the concession booths.''

For a minute I didn't get it. I asked, "Why was he?''

"Either one of two reasons, or both of them. To take the money out of the wallet and get rid of it. Or to keep on going over the outside fence of the park, to get out without having to go along the midway. Otherwise he might run into the Westphal boy again and maybe by then the wallet would have been missed, and if Obie knew Jimmy Chojnacki's record—''

"Did they know one another?"

"Probably. Anyway, they could have; Chojnacki had been in Westphal's class at South Side High. Expelled in the middle of his sophomore year, but that'd still give them a year and a half in the same class. They'd hardly have been friends but they must have known one another by sight."

"It's a pretty big school, but I guess they would. One of them famous in athletics and the other notorious for having been expelled; that's fame, too, isn't it? Did anyone see them together this morning at Whitewater?"

"How the hell would I know? We're leaving the Westphal kid out of the story so what does it matter?"

He went on over to his own desk and put paper in the typewriter.

I turned in the last of the upstate copy a few minutes after one o'clock. I could have made it last until two but Ed was giving me a break so I didn't try to stall. I stuck my head in his office and told him I was caught up.

"Good timing, Sam. Just got the word on a fire. Corner of Greenfield and Lassiter, on the south side. Get over there and phone in before deadline; you can knock off as soon as you've phoned."

I drove over in the ancient Buick—ten miles to the gallon and a quart of oil every time I get gas, but it gets me around—and got there just as the firemen were cleaning up. It hadn't been much of a fire. I found out who owned the building, the probable extent of the damage, how the fire had started and the fact that it was covered by insurance, and I went to the nearest tavern and phoned in.

It was only a quarter of two and I was free; my vacation had started. I could have gone home except for that phone call from Milly; she'd made it plain enough that she didn't want me to come home and drive her to the station. I had to kill an hour or two somehow.

I went to the bar and killed a few minutes of it by

drinking a beer. It tasted good and cooled me off a little but I didn't want a second one.

It came to me that I was only a few blocks from Whitewater Beach. I hadn't been there in years and there wasn't any reason why I shouldn't take a look at it again.

• 4 •

It was hot on the midway at Whitewater, but there were plenty of people there. No matter how hot it gets, an amusement park draws a crowd on Saturday afternoon. The Caterpillar, the Tilt-a-Whirl, the Comet and the Loop-the-Loop were all doing big business.

The Blue Streak was closed. A cop was standing in the space between it and the next concession where, by walking back a few yards and climbing a four-foot fence, you could enter the no-man's land between the concessions and the boundary fence, where the rides run. From one point on the midway you could see back, diagonally through the opening and over the fence, where some men were working at the bottom of the first dip of the roller coaster. There was a tight little knot of people standing at that spot peering back.

I showed my press pass to the cop and went on back, over the four-foot fence, to within a few yards of where the men were working.

It was muddy back there. Someone had played a hose over that part of the structure and tracks before the workmen had started; it wasn't hard to guess why.

The tracks, I saw, had already been straightened if anything had happened to them from the derailment. The men working now were two carpenters and one painter, the latter white-painting the boards almost before the

former finished nailing them down. They were almost
through. The wrecked car was gone, out of sight somewhere.

From where I stood I could see up the high steep hill
down which the car had come. I could picture it coming
down there like a bat out of hell, like a juggernaut, like
death, and the boy turning his head, seeing it coming . . .
I didn't like it. I had a hunch I might dream about it,
only it would be me there on the tracks.

The carpenters were moving away now, carrying their
tools and the painter took a final white swipe and then
he too, brush in one hand and can of paint in the other,
followed the carpenters. I stood a minute longer and then
I went back over the fence and back to the cop.

I asked him, "They going to run the ride again now?"

"Sure, soon as they get it fixed. Why not?"

"They've got it fixed now."

He looked back over his shoulder. "Yeah, guess they
have. Well, that lets me off."

He walked out onto the midway. The little knot of
people who'd been watching back over the fence was
dispersing now that there wasn't anything to watch back
there.

I wandered over to the front of the Blue Streak. There
was something I wanted to know, but I didn't know what
it was. Something, some question, at the back of my
mind that I couldn't get hold of and bring to the front.

A big, beefy man in a sailor straw hat was engaged
in tapping and studying the wheels of one of the two
cars up on the loading platform behind the vacant ticket
booth.

I stepped over a low gate and walked up beside him.
"Going to run today?" I asked him.

He put down the hammer in his hand and stood up.
He pushed the straw hat back on his forehead and looked
at me. "Yeah. Why?"

I gave him a quick flash of my press pass, just enough

so he could read the PRESS in big red letters but not enough to let him catch the name of the newspaper. If he knew about the enmity between the *Herald* and the park, he wouldn't feel like talking to a *Herald* man. "Associated Press," I told him. "Came around to cover the accident you had this morning."

"Wasn't our fault. Damn fool kid back where he had no business being. Going across the tracks, crazy like."

I nodded. "When did it happen?"

" 'Round ten, just getting ready to open up. Sent the first car around for the test run—we run each of 'em empty once every day before we start operating. And it happened. Car went up, started down the first hill and when it got to the bottom I heard it go off the track. First accident we ever had."

"Much damage? To the tracks and the car, I mean."

"Not too much. This is the car and we got it fixed up okay and they just finished the tracks a minute ago."

"Insured?"

"Yeah, sure, but it's going to hurt business. People hear there was an accident on the ride, they get afraid and don't ride it, don't stop to think it wasn't our fault and that the guy that got killed wasn't riding."

"You can't blame them," I said. "If there had been passengers in the derailed car they'd have been hurt."

"Yeah, there's that." He mopped his forehead with a handkerchief. "Guess you can't blame them. Besides, I'm losing four-five hours business on a Saturday."

"Were you the first one there after you heard the crash?"

"Yeah. Plenty of them there a few seconds after me, but I got there first. Look, mister, I got to keep working. My ticket seller and ride boy will be here in half an hour and by then I want to have run this car around a dozen times or so to be sure it's okay and the track's okay at the dip."

"Thanks," I said. "Guess I've got enough."

He was bent down tapping wheels again. He looked up. "Just remember it was the kid's own damn foolishness, not our fault."

"I'll remember," I told him.

I went back to the midway, wondering why I'd wasted time, wondering why I'd come here. Anyway, I'd killed enough time; it was three o'clock and I was on the opposite side of town from home. By the time I got there, unless I drove too fast, Millie would be gone. But why did I want to go home?

I walked out through the main gate and got into my car in the parking lot. It had been standing in full sunshine and it was baking hot even with all the windows run down.

I started driving and decided I was ready for another cold beer; I remembered that there was a tavern diagonally across from Haley's Funeral Parlor and that I'd be driving past there anyway. So I didn't drive past. I parked in front of the tavern and went in.

There wasn't any reason why I should be interested in Haley's or anything that went on there, but I found myself sipping my beer at the end of the bar next to the window where I had a good view of Haley's entrance.

I wondered if the Westphal family had been there yet to learn the good news they were going to learn, or already had learned, on their arrival. It was just about time for them to come. I ordered another beer and drank it slowly. I was just deciding whether to order a third when a big blue Chrysler sedan swung in to a jerky stop in front of Haley's. I recognized the man driving it from the picture of Armin Westphal I'd seen in the morgue file at the *Herald*. He was a big man, well dressed, with graying hair. His face looked frozen and expressionless.

There were two women in the car with him, all three of them in the front seat. I couldn't see them clearly until Westphal got out of the car on his side, went around and opened the door on their side. They got out and followed him toward Haley's entrance. The two women were about the same age; I judged that the one crying was Mrs. Westphal and the other, who held her arm and was talking to her, was the sister, Obie's aunt.

"Another beer, mister?" the bartender asked.

I told him, "Yeah, I guess so."

They were through the door and out of sight when I looked back. In about five minutes I saw them come out.

Westphal was walking stiffly, strangely, and his face hadn't changed at all; it still might have been carved out of ice. But the faces of the two women were radiant. Both of them seemed to be talking at once, excitedly. They were ahead; about halfway to the car one of them turned and said something to Westphal. He answered and smiled, but to me it looked as though the smile hurt him. And his face froze again as soon as the woman turned away.

They got into the car and drove off.

After a minute or two I went out and crossed the street to Haley's. I found Haley in his office but not, apparently, very busy. I looked around and asked, "Where's the girl? Grace Smith."

He smiled. "I sent her home. She threw a wingding when she learned the kid we got back there wasn't her crush after all. So happy she cried all over the place and then started a laughing jag. My God!"

"I happened to be having a beer across the street," I said. "I just saw the Westphals drive away."

He nodded. "Swell people and it was a break for me to be able to give somebody good news for once. *Real* people. Say, you know what Westphal's going to do?"

"What?"

"Pay for the other kid's funeral. Got me off on one side and wanted to know whether arrangements had been made. And when I told him what the circumstances were, he said to go ahead and he'd pay for it."

"What are the circumstances?"

"The Chojnackis? The kid's mother's a widow, works in a laundry. No money, and she didn't carry any insurance on the boy. She came here after the police had notified her. And after I'd talked with her I advised her to make arrangements with one of the cheaper morticians who could do the job so she wouldn't be mortgaging herself for the next five years paying it off. We're just not set up to provide inexpensive services." He frowned. "That reminds me. I'd better go around and see her right away—she hasn't got a phone—before she does make other arrangements."

"She's probably out doing that now."

"I don't think so. She was in pretty bad shape. I sent her home in a cab, and paid for the cab, and made her promise she'd stay home this afternoon. I told her there wasn't any hurry in making the transfer and that I wasn't charging her anything. Say, I forgot you were a reporter; I should have kept my mouth shut. Westphal asked me not to let anybody know he was paying for the funeral. You won't print it, will you?"

I shook my head. "I'm not even working. On vacation, starting an hour ago."

"Then what are you asking questions for?"

"Just curiosity. Happened to be in the neighborhood and, like I told you, I was having a beer across the street when I saw the Westphals leave here. But I'd got kind of interested in the case when I worked on it this morning so I thought I'd drop in a minute."

"Sure. Any time."

"Has the Westphal boy turned up yet?"

"About an hour ago. Missed his wallet and went to the lost-and-found at Whitewater. They figured he would and were waiting for him there. He went on home to wait for his parents."

"Why not here? They were coming here first."

He looked at me strangely. "Are you crazy? Think of

the shock if they walked in here and saw him alive, thinking him dead. People keel over for less than that. Better to let me break it to them first before they see him.''

"I'm stupid," I said.

"In my business you think of things like that, that's all. You get used to seeing people in shock and knowing how they act and how to handle them." He stood up. "Well, I don't want to push you out, but I've got to go see Mrs. Chojnacki. Got a car or can I drop you off anywhere?"

"Thanks," I said. "I've got a car."

I went out and got into it and drove home.

Home was an empty house. There was a note on the kitchen table in Millie's scrawly handwriting.

> Sam: Unless you want to open cans you'll have to eat out tonight. I gave away the bread and other things that were left that wouldn't keep. Don't change the setting on the refrigerator. Be sure all the doors and windows are locked when you leave and you'd better go to bed early tonight because don't forget Bill and Harvey are picking you up at five and you'll have to get up at four unless you do all your packing and everything tonight. Have a good time.

The chime clock on the mantel in the living room struck four times while I was reading. Millie would be on the train now and the train would be starting or about to start.

I decided I might as well get my packing over with right away. There wasn't much to do, just to throw some clothes into a suitcase and put it beside the front door. My fishing paraphernalia and my gun were ready, all cleaned and oiled and ready to use, and I put them by the suitcase. I even chose and laid out the clothes I was going to wear in the morning. Now I could sleep until a quarter of five and still be ready when they came. We'd stop for breakfast somewhere, we'd decided, after we were on the way.

I puttered around a while and then went out and drove to the nearest restaurant and had myself a dinner. It was not quite six when I'd finished and I sat there over coffee wondering if I should do something this evening. Even if I shorted myself a bit on sleep it seemed wasteful to spend the first evening of my vacation reading at home and early to bed.

Maybe I should call Nina Carberry. No, this wasn't the time to start anything like that. Or was it? Neither Millie nor I had done any playing around; however else either of us had failed it hadn't been that. But even if our being on the outs was temporary—in fact even more particularly if it turned out to be temporary—tonight would be my best and possibly only chance to stray a bit off the reservation at a time when it wouldn't put too much of a strain on my conscience. But no, I decided, it wouldn't be fair to Nina to pull a trick like that on her, strictly a one night stand at that. If Millie and I had already definitely broken up, things would be different; not that I'd have any intention of getting married again right away, but at least I'd be free. Besides I had no reason to believe that Nina would be even friendly if I called her or looked her up.

No, I might as well behave myself, go home and go to bed early, start my vacation trip with a full quota of sleep under my belt.

I went home, read a while, then went to bed and to sleep. I'd forgotten all about Jimmy Chojnacki and the roller coaster, and about Obie Westphal.

SUNDAY

· 1 ·

Part of my mind knew that I was dreaming. It was one of those borderline things between sleep and waking when you can think "This is only a dream" and still see and hear and feel vividly the things you know are not really happening.

I was lying face down across the tracks of a roller coaster, at ground level at the bottom of the first dip. I was able to move no part of me except my head; I could turn that to see the car that was rushing down the long steep incline toward me. There were three people in the front seat of the car; they were leaning over the railing watching me. They were the three I'd seen entering and leaving the funeral parlor, Mr. and Mrs. Westphal and the aunt. The two women were crying and laughing at the same time; the man's face was rigid and emotionless, a mask. The car passed over me and I felt nothing, I wasn't hurt. But one does not wonder in a dream, so I didn't wonder why I wasn't harmed and I didn't wonder how I knew that the next car would kill me. I lay there waiting for it, watching for it up that long slope of track, waiting to die. And fear grew into utter terror as I tried to move and couldn't, not even the muscles of my throat to scream.

I heard the sound of the car that had passed over me dying away in the distance, into silence. And then I heard a new sound.

I woke up fully. The new sound was the ticking of the alarm clock beside my bed, but it hadn't been that sound in my dream; it had been the clicking of a great ratchet. The sound you hear when a roller coaster car is being pulled up the first hill of its course; an endless chain pulls it up while a loudly clicking ratchet keeps it from sliding backward in case the chain should break. If you've ever ridden. or even watched, a roller coaster you've heard that sound.

I turned my head—as I had turned it in the dream, for I was lying face down in bed as I had lain face down across the track in my dream—and looked at the luminous hands and numbers of the clock on the night stand. It was five minutes after four o'clock; the alarm was set to go off in another twenty-five minutes, at four-thirty.

I burrowed my head back into the pillow and tried to sleep again, but I couldn't. I was wide and completely awake, although I usually waken slowly and groggily. I got up and shut off the alarm, knowing I might as well get up then as later.

I took a shower and dressed and then, because there was time to kill, I went down to the kitchen and made myself coffee. I had to drink it black because there wasn't any cream, but it tasted good.

I drank two cups of it, hot, black and sweet, and still had time to make a final round of the house, checking all the doors and windows, before the doorbell rang.

We got to Lake Laflamme a little before seven, with the day bright and clear and the sun just rising over the hills. It looked like a good day and a good time of day for fishing so we dumped our stuff in the Whelans' cottage, got the boat out of the boat house and went out on the lake right away without taking time to unpack anything but our fishing tackle.

By noon we had a nice string of perch and walleyes. It was hot as hell by then, out in the sun, and we figured that was our day's work, so we stayed on the screened-in porch all afternoon. We played two-bit limit stud and we drank cool Tom Collinses, lots of them.

When six o'clock came around none of us was in mood or shape to cook so we made some sandwiches and kept on playing poker while we ate them. We played another half hour or so until Harv—who was a bit out of practice at drinking—showed too strong a tendency to go to sleep among his chips. Bill and I shooed him to bed and made ourselves another drink.

Then, glasses in hand, we went down to the shore to watch the sun set across the lake. It was quite a sunset, like something out of Dante.

We sat there watching until the colors faded. My body was a bit drunk but my mind felt clear. Too clear.

I said, "Bill, maybe I should go back. I shouldn't have come."

He turned to look at me. "I know you've got something on your mind, Sam. You've been like a cat on a hot stove all day. If you really want to go back to town, Harv and I'll get along all right except that we'll have to play gin rummy instead of stud."

"I'd hate to spoil the week for you and Harv."

"You won't. But listen, Sam. Are you in trouble? Anything we can do?"

I shook my head.

"This is none of my business, but is it a woman?"

"No. Bill, it's something too screwy to explain. I'd sound crazy, even to myself, if I tried."

"Is it something you can maybe do quickly and get back while we're still here?"

I said, "It could be. It's something I've got to learn, to satisfy myself about. I might be able to do it in a day or it might take God knows how long. There's a bus runs near here, isn't there, Bill?"

"Sure. Stops at Holton, three miles from here. I think

there's a night bus, I mean a southbound one. Want me
to telephone and find out what time it leaves?''

We went back in and Bill Whelan called the bus
station.

He said, ''Leaves at ten. That's—let's see—about an
hour and a half from now. Want me to drive you in?''

''Thanks, no. A three-mile walk is just what I need
to sober up and do some thinking, and an hour and a
half is plenty of time for me to make it.''

''Okay, Sam. Listen, is there anything Harv or I can
do? If there is—''

''No, Bill, not a thing. Except—well, I don't want to
carry a suitcase three miles. Just keep all my stuff for
me and bring it back to town unless I do get back here
before the week is up. There's nothing in it I'll need
except my razor and toothbrush and I can carry them in
my pocket. And if I find I'm coming back I'll phone
you and let you meet me in Holton. Otherwise don't look
for me.''

I walked to Holton through bright moonlight and I was
sober when I got there, sober enough to wonder just how
big a fool I was making of myself.

But I took the bus.

MONDAY

· 1 ·

It was the damnedest thing, waking up that morning. I was in my own bed in my own house but everything was wrong. I wasn't supposed to be there. For awful seconds of disorientation I couldn't remember where I *was* supposed to be or why or what everything was all about.

Then it came back to me, and I didn't like it. I remembered the long walk, the bus ride, the taxi home from the bus station, unlocking the house and crawling into bed. But it seemed as ridiculous, as unmotivated, as though I'd dreamed it. Why in God's name had I spoiled a perfectly good vacation?

The clock told me that it was eight. That meant I'd had less than six hours' sleep—I hadn't got home until after two in the morning—but I was feeling so disgusted with myself that I knew I wouldn't be able to go back to sleep. I got up and dressed, and I made coffee and drank it.

When I felt whole and human again I telephoned the bus terminal and learned that there was only one bus a day to Holton; it left at four-fifteen and got there at eight-thirty. No use, I decided, phoning the Whelans now to ask them to meet it; they'd be out on the lake catching walleyes. I could phone them just before I left, or even from Holton after the bus got there. I might even decide to drive up in the Buick, although I knew I shouldn't; it had two tires ready to go at any moment and needed a general overhaul that I'd postponed until after vacation. In its present shape it was all right to drive around town where, at the worst, I might have to walk a few blocks to phone a garage, but it would be tempting fate to use it for a trip.

I decided I'd better wait till bus time. That gave me time to kill, about seven hours of it. Might as well start by going out for a breakfast since there wasn't anything in the house to eat. I got the Buick out of the garage and drove to a restaurant, picking up a paper—the *Journal*, the morning paper, not the *Herald*. I looked through it while I ate.

There wasn't any mention of Jimmy Chojnacki's accident in the *Journal*, but that wasn't surprising if nothing new had come up on it since Saturday; their Sunday paper would have covered the story and, since they had no grudge against Whitewater Beach, there was no reason for them to keep it alive unless there were further developments.

I wondered, though, how their yesterday's paper had handled it and whether they'd dug any facts that we'd missed, so I asked the waitress if there still happened to be a Sunday *Journal* around. She looked in a pile of papers under the counter and found one for me. The story, when I found it, was only six column inches on page two. It didn't have anything I didn't already know except the Chojnacki boy's address. It was 2908 Radnik Street, which would be within a block or two of the back entrance of Whitewater Beach, which meant he'd probably hung around there a lot.

Back in the Buick I looked at my watch and decided what the hell; now that I had been silly enough to come back to town I might as well do at least a few of the things I'd wanted to do, as many of them as I could before bus time. Maybe I could convince myself finally and completely that there wasn't anything back of my wild hunch.

I drove south to Radnik Street. Back of Whitewater it runs through the area known as Southtown, a tough, shabby district. It had been a red light district a good many years ago. The city had cleaned that up, but it was still a rough place, centering around one block, the 3100 block of Radnik Street, that was a Bowery or South State Street in miniature, with taverns, bums, drunks and all the trimmings.

I found 2908 and it was a three-story tenement with sixteen mailboxes in the narrow dark hallway. I found the name Chojnacki on a rusty box numbered 306 so I went up the stairs to the third floor, found the right door and knocked.

The door opened quickly. For what must have been at least two seconds the woman who opened it and I stared at one another and my expression must have been even more surprised than hers. Then I said, "*Nina*, what on earth—?"

She put a finger to her lips. "Shh. Just wait a minute right here. I'll be out and explain." She closed the door quietly.

I knew there must be some explanation but I couldn't think of a logical one. And explanation or no it was the damnedest thing. I'd been thinking about Nina Carberry, had almost called her evening before last—and now I'd knocked on Mrs. Chojnacki's door and Nina had opened it.

And now she opened it again; this time she came out and closed it behind her. Then she turned to me. "You wanted to see Mrs. Chojnacki, Sam?"

"Yes. What are *you* doing—?"

"Social service work. Sam, you can't see her right now. I just got her to sleep—she's slept hardly at all since it happened and she needs sleep. Do you have paper and pencil?"

"Sure. Why?"

"Print 'Do Not Disturb' on a piece of paper and I'll

pin it on the door. I've got a pin. Then if anyone else comes around they won't wake her up.''

I did the printing on a leaf of a notebook and handed it to her as I tore it out. She had a pin, from somewhere, in her hand by then, and put the paper on the door with it.

She turned back to me. ''You're still working for the *Herald*, Sam? I suppose you wanted to interview her. But maybe I can tell you whatever you want to know. I know Mrs. Chojnacki pretty well, and I knew Jimmy, ever since he started high school.''

''Fine,'' I said. ''And we've got more to talk about than that. After all these years. Where can we go to talk? And is it too early in the morning to suggest a drink?''

She looked at her wrist watch. ''Well—half past ten *is* a little early, but I wouldn't mind having one. I've a few more calls to make today but I guess I can make them this afternoon just as well.''

''Hmmm,'' I said. ''Inviting yourself to lunch too. Okay, it's a deal. But before we take off, wait a minute. Let me look at you.''

I stepped back and looked. Six years had done a lot for Nina. She'd been a pretty girl; now she was a beautiful woman. Almost beautiful, at least. The dark horn-rimmed glasses gave her just a touch of primness, a schoolteacherish look. But her body didn't look schoolteacherish, not by miles. It had filled out, and in the right places and to the right degree, since I'd last seen her.

I said, ''How do you dare come in a neighborhood like this one wearing a sweater like that?''

She smiled, or maybe I should say she grinned, a gamin grin. ''The glasses protect me.''

''Take them off.''

''Not on your life, Sam. I'd say I need protection right now, the way you're looking at me.''

''Maybe you do at that,'' I said. ''All right, I've looked

my fill, for the moment. Where would you like to go for that drink?''

· 2 ·

We settled on the cocktail lounge at the Statler. We went there in Nina's coupe instead of my car because she'd left hers in a limited-parking zone and would have had to move it anyway.

Over Manhattans, I said, ''You can take off the glasses now. We're in a public place and the bartender is watching.''

She smiled and took them off.

''You *are* beautiful,'' I said. ''Nina, how come you've never married? Or *have* you?''

She shook her head. ''No I haven't. But as to why, it's a long and dull story. Let's skip it—for now, anyway. You're still a reporter for the *Herald?*''

''Yes, but I don't do much leg work any more. Mostly rewrite, on the city desk. And an occasional sob story.''

''Is that why you were looking up Mrs. Chojnacki?''

I hesitated, and then decided to tell her the truth, or at least a little of it.

''No, I'm on vacation this week. It's just—well, I helped cover the story Saturday when it broke and I got interested, curious about a point or two. I'm afraid I'd have told Mrs. Chojnacki I was interviewing her for the paper, but I wouldn't have been.''

''Don't go back there today, please, Sam. She's pretty upset and, outside of her own friends of course, the fewer people she has to talk to the better. Or tomorrow either; the funeral's tomorrow, at two o'clock. Let me answer any questions that I *can* answer, about her or Jimmy, meanwhile. What do you want to know?''

I said, "I'm not sure just what I do want to know. Just tell me things."

"Well—I started doing social service work three years ago; that was about the time Jimmy was just entering high school, South Side High."

"Wait," I said. "I don't want to interrupt you about the Chojnackis, but are you still working in the office at the high school or are you doing social service work full time?"

"I still work at the high school. But that's not too much of a job—it's only six hours a day, five days a week."

"And nine months out of the year. Or do you work there summers, too?"

"Oh yes, summers too. They have a summer term— for students who want to make up subjects they've flunked in. Or sometimes to skip a grade or to take vocational subjects they can't work into their regular schedules. And of course they have to keep the office running too. I'm not working there today because it's a school holiday. Dr. Bradshaw is in town."

"Who the hell is Dr. Bradshaw?"

"Just about the top authority in secondary education in the country; he travels for the National Board of Education to keep teachers all over the country abreast of the trends in educational methods. He's holding a forum here today and every teacher who's in town is supposed to attend."

I said, "Good for Dr. Bradshaw then. Otherwise you'd be working at the school right now and I wouldn't have run into you. Which, in itself, is an amazing coincidence."

"Why a coincidence? I mean, it's almost strange that we've lived in the same city for the last five years—or is it six?—and *haven't* happened to meet somewhere or other."

I said, "I guess so," and let it go at that because I didn't want to tell her, not yet anyway, that I'd been thinking about her and had almost telephoned her just night before last. "But go on, tell me about the social service work—since you've started—before we get back to the Chojnacki business."

"There isn't much to tell, about that. I've always done some kind of part-time work along with my thirty hours a week at the school; that's not really a full-time job. Three years ago I learned that the Social Service Agency here took on part-time workers and I thought I'd like it so I took a job with them."

"Do you still like it?"

"Yes. You see a lot of the seamy side, of course, unpleasant things, but it gives you a good feeling to be helping people who need help. The pay is pretty nominal but with my school job it lets me make out. And a good thing about it, from the practical standpoint, I don't have to work any specified hours. I'm assigned a certain number of families to keep in touch with and help, and I'm supposed to see each family once a week—at least for a few minutes just to keep in touch with them, longer if they need any help I can give—but I can do it afternoons, evenings, Saturdays, any time I want."

"Sounds like a good deal," I said. "All right, now the Chojnackis."

"They were one of the first families I was assigned to, and they've been on my list ever since. There's just Mrs. Chojnacki left now; there were three Chojnackis three years ago. Her husband, Stanley—probably originally Stanislaus, since he was born in Poland—was a drunkard. Not the vicious or cruel type, just weak. But he couldn't hold a job and couldn't keep from spending any money he did get on drinking. They almost never had enough to eat despite the fact that Anna—that's Mrs. Chojnacki's first name and I call her that by now—

worked as much as her health would let her, more than she should have, for that matter. Stanley died two years ago. Of pneumonia.

"Anna has done a little better since then than before. Her health has been a little better—although she's far from being a well woman—and she's been able to work more hours at the laundry. She and Jimmy had enough to eat, if not anything over. Probably she'd have been taken off my list except for her troubles with Jimmy. Do you know about that?"

"I know he had a record for stealing and picking pockets."

Nina nodded. "And it was almost as though he just couldn't *help* stealing whenever he had a chance. He was a good kid in every other way, not mean or belligerent. Good to his mother—except for the hurt it caused her to have him in and out of reform school and—and being what he was. It wasn't so much that he needed money, although there was that, too; Anna wasn't able to give him any pocket money."

"Did he try working?"

"Lots of times, but he just couldn't hold a job for long. He had a kind of fierce independence that made it hard for him to take orders or to take any reprimand he didn't think he deserved. And whether he was working or not—this is why I'm sure it wasn't just a matter of money—he'd steal. And every time he'd lose a job for stealing from his employer it was harder for him to get another job next time."

"Doesn't sound like a very nice kid," I said.

"That's the funny thing about it, Sam. He *was* a nice kid in spite of the way that makes him sound. And a smart one, too. He got excellent grades in school—I checked his record at elementary school when I started working with the Chojnackis, and of course I had access to his records at South Side High while he was a freshman there and he was doing wonderfully well—scholasti-cally—right up to the time he was expelled. For being caught rifling clothes in the locker room of the gym.

"And he really wanted an education. He spent most of his evenings reading, and not reading just junk. I've seen lots of the books he brought home from the public library—history, biography, literature. And grammar and composition. Sam, he spoke flawless English, better than mine, and he came from a home where only Polish or very broken English was spoken. He wanted to write."

"I'll be damned," I said. "Listen, do you happen to know whether he went to Whitewater alone Saturday morning, or whether he was with someone?"

"No. Why does that matter?"

"I'm not sure that it does. Do you know who his friends were?"

"I—I'm afraid I don't know that either."

"You don't happen to know whether he knew a boy named Westphal?"

"*Obie* Westphal?"

"Yes."

"Why—they must have known one another by sight; they were in the same class at South Side. But they wouldn't have been friends."

"Why not? I know they're from different social strata, but if Jimmy was as literate as you say, that might not have mattered."

"But—they wouldn't have had any interest in com-mon, Sam. None at all. Obie gets good grades in school, but he isn't *interested* in studying or reading as Jimmy was. And Obie's wonderful in athletics and Jimmy hated anything like athletics. Probably because he was small and not very strong, not able to compete in anything that took strength. And—oh, they were as different in every other way as their backgrounds were different. No, they might have known one another slightly—I don't know about that—but they certainly wouldn't have been friends. There wouldn't have been any one common interest to bridge all the differences. Why do you ask about Obie?''

"Jimmie had Obie Westphal's wallet in his pocket when he was killed. He must have lifted it shortly before."

"*Sam!*" Nina looked frightened. "That isn't going to be in the paper, is it?"

"No. Not in the *Herald*, anyway. We knew that before we went to press the first day and didn't run it then so there's no reason why we should now. And the same goes for the *Journal*, I guess. I read how they handled it Sunday—the story broke too late for their Saturday morning paper—and they didn't mention the wallet. They must have known."

"Thank God for that. Mrs. Chojnacki mustn't ever find that out. It would almost kill her."

"Why? I mean, she knew Jimmy stole. So why would one more time matter?"

"Because—well, Anna is deeply religious, Sam. And it happens that Jimmy hadn't been in any trouble—hadn't stolen anything, as far as she knew—for two months or so before he died. And her one big consolation in what happened, the thing that keeps her from going to pieces completely, is that she can think he'd reformed, that he 'died good,' she put it, that's the idea she clings to. And if she ever learns he died just after stealing again, with the stolen property right on him—"

"I can see that," I said. "Not that I'm religious myself, but I can see how that would be important to someone who is. Okay, Nina, she won't learn from me. And if the police didn't tell her that right away, when she was notified about the accident, I don't think they ever will."

"Oh, I hope not. That's the thing that keeps her going, the consolation of believing he died a good boy. And too, he'll have a nice funeral; that means a lot to people like Anna. The amusement park is paying for it."

"They are?"

"It must be the park because Anna told me someone is paying for it and doesn't want his name known. I told her it must be the park management—or possibly the concessionaire who runs the roller coaster—and the reason they're doing it anonymously is that it might seem like they admitted responsibility if they did it openly. It wouldn't matter—I mean, Anna realizes they're *not* responsible and she wouldn't sue. But they couldn't be sure of that."

I considered telling her who was really paying for the funeral and then decided not to. I'd promised Haley I wouldn't tell and there wasn't any good reason for breaking that promise to tell Nina. In fact, it might be better if she and Mrs. Chojnacki kept on thinking what they thought now.

"What time is it, Sam?"

I looked at my watch. "A few minutes after twelve. Afternoon. It's legal to have a drink now; want another one?"

"Thanks, Sam. I don't think I'd better. Are you hungry enough to have some lunch?"

We moved to the coffee shop for lunch and then Nina said she'd better get back and finish her remaining calls.

She double-parked beside the Buick when I pointed it out to her. I opened the door on my side but I didn't get out yet.

I asked, "Where are you living, Nina?"

"I have an apartment near the school."

"Are you in the phone book?"

She looked at me for a long moment. "You're still married, aren't you, Sam?"

"I'm married, yes. But I still want to know."

"But it's no good for us to see one another again if—"

I didn't help her.

"Well—you can *look* in the phone book and see, can't you?"

I grinned at her and got out of the car. "Might do that sometime. 'By, Nina."

I had to close the door quickly because the car was starting.

I watched it around the corner and wondered if I'd ever call her. Not whether I wanted to, but whether I would.

Back in the Buick I sat behind the wheel a minute or two and then I drove the few blocks to Whitewater Beach. That was one of the places I'd intended to go; I might as well now while I was so near.

There weren't many adults there, but the midway was full of kids. As I walked back toward the Blue Streak I passed the fence over which Jimmy must have climbed, and over which I myself had climbed Saturday afternoon. There was an addition to it now, three strands of barbed wire atop it, spaced four or five inches apart. They weren't taking chances, anymore, of kids getting across that fence into the area beyond.

A girl was in the ticket office of the roller coaster, but she hadn't opened the window yet; she was counting out change and bills and putting them into the compartmented change drawer.

Up on the starting platform the same big beefy man in the straw hat was going over the seats of one of the two cars with a feather duster.

He turned as he heard me coming. "You again. What this time?"

I grinned at him. "Nothing much this time. Think I'll take a ride today. Press privilege, or do I buy a ticket?"

He grunted. "Buy a ticket. We'll be open in five, ten minutes. Soon as I run each car around once."

"You're opening later today."

"Weekday. Two o'clock weekdays. Ten o'clock Saturdays, Sundays, holidays. Look, what's the big idea? You trying to *make* something of that accident?"

I shook my head. "Thinking of writing a story about roller coasters."

"Oh." He thought that over a minute. "Well, put in it how safe they are. That Saturday business was the first accident *mine* ever had, and the only ones I've heard of on others have been where people do something crazy like standing up in the car or leaning over the edge of it. We're safer than railroads. A hell of a lot safer than automobiles."

"I'll put that in," I said. "Did you find a fountain pen around here Saturday afternoon?"

He shook his head. "Nope. Lose one?"

"I had it not long before I talked to you and missed it just after I left the park. Say, I'll bet I know where I dropped it. I was watching the workmen fix up the track back where the car went off and was bending over looking at it. I'll bet that's when it fell out of my pocket. I'll go back and look there."

I stepped down off the side of the platform. He said, "Hey," and I turned. He said, "I'm not going to run the cars while you're back there, so don't take long."

"Don't be silly," I told him. "I'm not going to be *on* the tracks; I'm not crazy. And it may take me awhile to look around in that high grass. Go ahead and start when you're ready."

I walked on back along the tracks, past the high scaffolding of the first big hill, the up slope and the down slope. When I got to the place where the tracks came down to ground level I stopped and, a few feet back from the tracks, bent down and pretended, in case anyone was watching, to be looking for something in the high grass.

A minute or two passed and then I heard it, the clicking ratchet sound I'd heard in my dreams, the sound of a car being pulled up the incline toward the top. It was *loud*, just as loud as it had been in my dreams Sunday morning.

Nobody could possibly have failed to hear it, nobody who wasn't deaf or nearly so. And Nina would have mentioned deafness, if there'd been any, when she was telling me about Jimmy; physical handicaps of any sort would surely be mentioned by a social worker describing a case.

The car was coming over the top now and the clicking stopped, but instead there was a gathering roar of sound that made me take a step back although where I'd been standing was a safe distance, four feet away. The sound crescendoed and maybe it was imagination but the very ground under my feet seemed to shake as it went past and shot up the hill beyond.

I was shaking a little myself whether the ground under me had or not.

And I knew now, for sure, what I'd suspected—*one* of the things I'd suspected—all along. The death of Jimmy Chojnacki hadn't been an accident.

I couldn't picture it that way at all.

But I could picture two boys standing back here together, hearing that ratchet and knowing a car was coming, standing deliberately close to the track for the thrill of it, but still a safe distance back. And just as the car starts down the hill I could see one of the boys, the bigger and huskier of the two, taking a quick look back toward the midway to be sure nobody was watching through the one narrow space through which it was possible for them to be seen and then, just as the car roared to the bottom of the hill, giving the smaller boy a push that sent him sprawling face down and arms out in front of him, flat across the tracks.

That I could picture, and it haunted me.

I'd wanted it to go away but it hadn't. It had grown instead until it had driven me back to town from Lake Laflamme to try to prove that I was wrong—or right. Until now it had just been a hunch—oh, a hunch based on bits of conscious and unconscious knowledge, as all hunches are—but now it was more than that. I knew, or at least I thought that I knew.

I heard the clicking of the ratchet again. The other car was starting around now. I didn't want to stay there and see and hear it go by so I went back to the platform along the scaffolding of the hill.

"Find your pen?"

I shook my head.

"Well, look, if that *is* where you lost it, maybe the painter found it back there when he went back to put on the second coat. And he might have turned it in to lost-and-found. Might as well ask there."

"I will," I said. "Thanks. That would be where the main office is, back of the bandstand?"

"Yeah. Say, if you're really going to write a piece on roller coasters—and give us a break in it—forget what I said about buying a ticket. Ride all you want to. Here— get in this car now."

"Thanks, but I'll come back later when you've started drawing business. I want to have other people riding too so I can watch their reactions."

"See you later then."

·3·

The Lost and Found Department was a window in the side of the wooden building that housed the office of the amusement park, not a window with glass in it but with a wooden door that opened inward. The window was closed but there was a bell button beside it and lettered over the button as an instruction, "Ring Bell."

I rang bell.

A few seconds later the window opened and a young man with red hair and freckles looked at me through it.

I flashed the press card. "Were you on duty at the window here Saturday?"

"Up to five o'clock, yeah. Someone else was on in the evening."

"I want to ask you about a billfold that was turned in with identification showing that it belonged to a Henry O. Westphal. Do you remember it?"

"I remember *about* it. It wasn't turned in, exactly."

"What happened?"

"Well, somewhere around noon—I don't remember the exact time but it was before I went for lunch at half past twelve, Gilman came around. Gilman's the cop who's on duty here days. He wanted to know if a kid named Westphal had inquired here about a wallet and I told him no. He said, 'He probably will as soon as he misses it and when he does tell him to look me up; I've got it for him. I'll be over near the Blue Streak for a while.' So I asked him why he didn't just leave the wallet here for the kid, and he told me he had something to tell the kid along with giving him the wallet.

"So about ten or fifteen minutes after I'm back from lunch—I just hang out a sign 'Window Closed, Back at 1:30' while I'm out—the bell rings and it's the kid asking about his wallet and I send him to Gilman, and that's all I know about it."

"Thanks," I said. "Do you know if Gilman's around now?"

"He'd be on duty, yeah, but I don't know just where he'd be. Somewhere around the park."

A blue uniform is easy to spot and I spotted one walking down the midway a few minutes later. I caught up to it and found that it contained the policeman I'd seen, and had shown my press pass to, when he'd been guarding the fence over which I'd climbed to watch the workmen finish the track repair Saturday.

"Officer Gilman?" I asked him.

"Yeah. You're the reporter that was around Saturday, ain't you?"

I admitted it. I told him what I wanted to know.

He told me, "Somewhere around twelve Lieutenant Grange comes here from the funeral parlor and gives me the wallet. He says it was on the kid that was killed that morning but that it wasn't his wallet, see? The dead kid was a pickpocket and he must have lifted it. So the right owner, Henry O. Westphal was the name in the wallet, would miss it and come around asking at the office probably. And he explained what had happened about the mistaken identification and about the Westphal kid's parents being notified and—do you know about that part of it?"

I told him that I did.

"Well, he wanted me to explain things, what had happened, to the kid and tell him to go home and wait for his ma and pa there, because they'd want to see him and reassure themselves kind of after a false alarm like that.

"So I kept the wallet and left word with Red over at the Lost and Found Department to send the kid to me if he asked there. So Red sent the kid over and I gave him the wallet and the message. That's all there was to it."

"Did he say anything about how he'd lost the wallet, whether he knew it had been stolen and not just lost, anything like that?"

"No. What difference does that make?"

"None, I guess. Did you happen to look in the wallet to see how much money was in it?"

"No, but the Lieutenant told me. He said there was fifteen bucks in the wallet and I took his word for it. He says I should ask the boy how much was in when he lost it, just to check. So I did and he said fifteen bucks all right."

"I wonder why he didn't miss it sooner," I said. "It

must have been stolen before ten and he didn't miss it till after one-thirty.''

''Wondered a little about that myself and we were talking so I asked him. He said he'd left the park not much after ten and had driven downtown, that he hadn't tried to spend any money except change until he tried to pay for his lunch. He drove right back to the park but the window was closed so he had to kill time and go back after half past one. Well, that's all there was to it, except he said he'd go home right away and I guess he did.''

On my way out of the park I stopped at a phone booth and used the directory to look up the Westphals' address, which I'd forgotten since Saturday morning. It wasn't too far, about two miles. It would be in the Oak Hill district, a good residential neighborhood despite the fact that it's bounded on one side by the freight yards.

I didn't call the phone number, although I made a note of it in case I wanted to call it sometime. Right now I wanted a look at Obie Westphal if I could get one without having him see me or know that I was looking at him. I didn't want to talk to him yet.

I drove there, past the house. It was a nice-looking place, newly painted and with a big, well-kept yard surrounded by a white picket fence. It was a big house, too, at least ten rooms; if only Mr. and Mrs. Westphal and Obie lived there, they had plenty of space.

I U-turned in the next block and came back; I parked on the opposite side of the street facing the house and two doors down so I could sit there and watch through the windshield. All the houses in the block were set back about the same distance from the street so from where I parked I could see the front and one side of the house and more than half of the yard.

I sat there and nothing happened; no one left or entered the house. Someone was there, though, either Mrs. Westphal or a maid or housekeeper; once I saw a dust mop shaken from an upstairs window. I looked at my watch after a while and it was four o'clock. The bus was leaving now that would have taken me back to Lake Laflamme, and I wasn't on it. I wondered if I'd get back there at all.

At half past five Mr. Westphal came home in the blue Chrysler sedan I'd seen him driving Saturday afternoon. He left it at the curb in front of the house and went inside.

At half past six lights went on inside the house and half an hour later they went off again and Mr. and Mrs. Westphal came out of the house together; they got in the car and drove away.

I drove past the house slowly, making sure there wasn't a light on anywhere. I'd wasted about four hours; obviously Obie wasn't home and hadn't been home.

So I kept on going, but I didn't try to follow the Westphal car. I was almost starving by then so I headed for the nearest business street and found myself a restaurant. I got my order in and then went to the phone booth.

It was about time I quit thinking about only one aspect of what I suspected and took a look at it whole.

I dialed the number of the *Journal* and asked for Don Thaley. Don is a closer friend of mine than anyone on the *Herald;* I could trust him farther than any of my fellow reporters. Besides, the city room of the *Herald* would be closed now, but the *Journal* is a morning paper and Don would be working now and since he wasn't a leg man he'd probably be in.

He was.

"Don? This is Sam Evans. How's everything?"

"Fine. Hey, I thought you were on vacation and supposed to be out of town."

"I am. On vacation, I mean. But something came up that brought me back to town, something personal."

"Do I know her?"

"Quiet, please. Don, I want you to get me some dope from your morgue and then forget I asked you for it. For reasons of my own I don't want to go to the *Herald* for this."

"Sure, Sam. What is it?"

"I want the dope on the four—I think it's four—fatal accidents that happened at South Side High in the last few years. Names, dates, and anything else. One was a boy who fell out of the tower window, one was a boy who slipped and hit his head on something, I forget what, and there were two drownings in the pool. One of them was a teacher."

"Good Lord, what do you want all that for?"

"I'm checking up on what's probably a wild idea. And I don't want to talk about it until and unless I get something. But if you'll dig that dope for me it gives a drink at Murphy's, first chance we get to meet there."

"Okay, no questions asked. But, Sam, I don't know offhand how I could get it for you right away. There must be a story on each of those cases in our morgue but they'd be separate, each under the name of the victim of the accident, and not cross-indexed under South Side High. I remember a couple of the accidents, wrote the stories myself from dope I got over the telephone, but that was a year or so ago; I don't remember the names now."

"Is there anyone there who might remember them?"

"Hmmm. I doubt it, not any one person anyway. If I canvass the office I might get all or most of the names."

"No, don't do that. I'll get it somewhere. Thanks anyway."

"Your best bet would be someone who works at the school, a teacher maybe, or anyone who's worked there the last several years. They might remember the names and if you can give me the names I can dig the rest for you. Don't you know anyone who works there?''

"Sure," I said. "I should have thought of that."

Not that I hadn't. I'd thought of calling Nina, of course, but I guess I'd been afraid to.

I went back to the counter and ate. Then I went back to the phone booth, looked up Nina's number and called her. She was home.

"This is Sam, Nina. Are you doing anything?"

"Why no, but—Sam, hadn't we better drop this? It was nice seeing you again today. But you're married."

"Okay," I said. "Maybe you're right, Nina. But there's something I want to ask you. How many fatal accidents have there been at South Side High in the last few years?"

"Three—no, four. Why?"

"Do you remember the names of all of the persons who were killed?"

"I think so. The teacher was Constance Bonner. The boy who fell from the tower window was named Green—Greenough, I think, but I can't remember his first name. The Negro boy who was killed in the locker room was William Reed. And the girl who was drowned—no, I can't think of her name, Sam. That was two years ago and she was a freshman then; she'd just signed in and I didn't have many records on her so I don't remember. Is it important, Sam?"

"It is to me. Do you know where I could find out?"

"Why, I guess I can find out for you by looking it up in my diary. I keep a sort of journal, day-by-day stuff. I suppose it's a silly thing to do but—Well, if I hunt back I can find the entries I made when each of those accidents happened. But it'll take a little while to find them."

"Can you take time now to do that? And I'll call you back in half an hour, an hour, whenever you say. How long do you think it'll take you to find them?"

"I don't know. I might hit the right entries right away

or it might take me—Oh, come on around, Sam, since you really—I mean, I thought you—''

I grinned at the mouthpiece of the telephone. "Okay, Nina. And we might as well have a drink while I'm there. What shall I bring a bottle of?''

"Anything you want.''

"That sounds bad. As though you drink anything and everything. How'd you go for Manhattans again?''

"Fine. And I happen to have a bottle of vermouth and some maraschino cherries; you can bring just the whisky.''

"The vital ingredient. Okay, be seeing you.''

I'd forgotten to ask her address so I had to look up the listing in the phone book again. It was on South Howell Street, a number that would be a few blocks west of South Side High.

I knew Nina would be curious as to why I wanted the information and I wasn't ready to talk to anybody yet about what I suspected, so I got a story ready on the way over.

The address was an apartment building, nice-looking but not swanky. I found Nina's name and pushed the button beside it, then caught the door as the lock clicked.

Nina opened the door to my knock. She wasn't wearing her glasses, and she was beautiful. Dark brown hair neatly but not precisely waved; it looked soft and touchable. Oval face with skin like a schoolgirl's, even to a few faint freckles on the nose; full lips, smiling, parted just enough to show the edges of perfect teeth, parted just enough to be perfect for kissing. A quilted silk housecoat molded the curves of her body.

She closed the door behind me. "I haven't looked it up yet, Sam. I'd just finished eating when you called and I wanted to do the dishes and straighten up the place.''

"No hurry. Let's make a drink first." I handed her the bottle I'd bought. "You know where things are, so I'll let you make the first one.''

"All right, but you can help by breaking out a tray of ice cubes. I guess you can find them."

I guessed that I could, since the refrigerator was in plain sight in the alcove of the room that formed a kitchenette. It was a one-room apartment but a largish room, nicely furnished. Wall-to-wall carpeting in beige that matched the upholstery of the chair and sofa, matching walnut in the wooden pieces, walls papered in unfigured tan. A room in shades of brown, an attractive, peaceful room.

We made drinks and sat down with them, I on the sofa and she on the matching chair, a safe six feet distant.

"Nina," I said, "I'm really curious why you haven't married. You said it was a long story—but unless it's something you don't want to tell me—"

"It's not *really* a long story, unless I wanted to go into detail about every man I've known. I've had chances to marry, several times. But none of them—well, none of them happened to be anyone I thought I'd be satisfied to spend a lifetime with. Probably I was too fussy—and will end up an old maid because of it."

"I doubt it. But don't tell me that you haven't—" I didn't quite know how to put it, but she spared me from trying.

"Had any affairs? A few, Sam. I haven't been promiscuous, but I haven't been completely celibate all the time. I'm human. But any time it's happened it's been more than—than—"

"A romp in the hay?"

She laughed. "Yes, more than a romp in the hay. Maybe that's what's wrong with most men; they think sex is only that."

"Maybe that's what's wrong with most women," I said; "they think sex must necessarily be more than that. Not that it can't be. But even hay is nice stuff."

She laughed again. "Let's not fight a skirmish in the war between the sexes. Sam, you make us another drink—

now that the ingredients and paraphernalia are out on the sink where you can find them—while I see what I can find about those accidents in my journals. But—why are you interested in them?''

I said, "I'm writing an article, something I hope to sell to a magazine, and I want to finish it this week while I'm on vacation. You've heard of accident prones, haven't you?''

"People who keep having accidents? Of course. The current theory, I think, is that subconsciously they want to die; they have a death wish that their conscious mind isn't aware of.''

"Right. Well, my article is going to try to prove—partly seriously, partly facetiously—that the current theory is wrong because there are buildings as well as people that are accident prone. And a building hasn't *got* a subconscious mind.''

"Buildings? Are you out of your mind, Sam?''

"Maybe out of my subconscious one. But it happens to be a fact, Nina; there *are* buildings that have more accidents happen in them than the law of averages allows. And not because they're badly designed or dangerous in themselves. It's just that they're prone to have accidents happen in them.''

"Sam, that's crazy.''

"Maybe it is—and that's why I'm writing it as though I'm writing tongue in cheek, whether I am or not. But I've got a lot of data on buildings that have had considerably more than their share of accidents. And I want to add South Side High to my roster.''

"But—four accidents in three years. That's not so awfully many.''

"Isn't it? Four *fatal* accidents? There are three other high schools in town, all about the same size as South. Each of those three is over twenty years old and two of them never had a fatal accident. The other had *one*, about five years ago, and that happened on the football field;

kid had his neck broken in scrimmage. South Side's the newest of the four, about fifteen years old, and it's had four fatal accidents, and all of them within the last three years.''

"But it didn't have any before. Doesn't that prove—?''

"It proves, if anything, that it became accident prone three years ago. Accident prones among people aren't born that way; they become accident prone at some time in their lives.''

"Sam, that's such a weird idea that it really might make a good article—for a Sunday supplement anyway. All right, make those drinks and I'll get my journals.''

I made the drinks and when I came back with them she was sitting with three largish volumes, the size of ledgers, on her lap; one of them open. I could see that it was handwritten, in the small neat handwriting that I now remembered from our high school days. Each of those three books, presumably one each year for the last three years, must have contained a hundred thousand words or so if it was filled.

She closed the opened one as she took the drink I handed her. "I've found two of them already, Sam, the first two; they both happened three years ago. The boy who fell out of the tower window was the first one.''

"Tell me about it.''

"I was right about the name, Wilbur Greenough. He was a freshman.'' She shivered a little. "I remember that one well because it was the first serious accident I'd ever seen, the first dead body I'd ever seen—except at a funeral, of course.''

"You mean you actually saw it happen?''

"No, but I *heard* it, and I saw him right afterwards. He fell from one of the front tower windows and landed on the front steps. I was working at my desk—the school offices are still in the same place, on the first floor front— and I heard a noise outside that sounded like—well, a hard thud. Then I heard a girl scream and I ran to the open window and looked out, and he was lying there on the steps. And it was awful—his head had hit and cracked open and there was blood and—''

I saw that wasn't doing her any good, so I said, "Skip that part if you want, Nina. Was there any investigation made?''

"Yes, of course. But it didn't bring out much. Nobody saw him fall—until he landed, that is. It was during second lunch period, near the end of the period; he'd already eaten. He must have gone up into the tower and either leaned too far out of the window looking down or else climbed out on the ledge. There's a six-inch ledge along the row of three windows. And all three of the windows were open; he might have climbed out of one and tried walking along the edge to come in at another window. They found out that other boys had done that.''

"Were any other students up there in the tower room with him?''

"Apparently not; at least they never found out that there were any other boys up there at the time. Since then the door to the tower has been kept locked, unless it's actually in use. And that isn't often. The Drama Club uses it for rehearsals and the school band practices up there; that's about all. It's unlocked only when either of those groups is scheduled to use it.

"That was in late September, not long after school had started. And the next accident was in January, the Negro boy who fell in the locker room. His name was William Reed. I didn't put any details about it into my journal, but I guess there wasn't much to put down. Nobody knows just how he fell because he was alone in the locker room at the time, as far as they could find out, but he'd hit his head on the sharp corner of a bench. He wasn't found for several hours.''

"Several *hours*? Good Lord, how could he lie there that long?''

"It was the last period and he was about the last, or one of the last ones getting dressed; he'd taken a shower after gym—probably didn't have a tub or shower at home and took a long one. And his locker was in the last row back; even if there were a few boys left dressing in other rows they wouldn't have passed him on their way out. The janitor found him when he got around to sweeping in the locker room."

"Investigation again?"

"*All* the accidents were investigated. But since nobody saw the accident happen, there wasn't much they could find out. There was a recommendation made that the benches be replaced with ones with rounded edges and I think it was done; I'm not sure."

"And the next one, the freshman girl who drowned, was two years ago? Will it be hard for you to find that one?"

"No, because I'm pretty sure it happened right after school started and that gives me about the right date, so I may find it quickly."

She'd put her drink down on the coffee table and was leafing through another of the books. After a few minutes she said, "Here it is. Oh yes, her name was Bessie Zimmerman. I didn't put down much about it because I didn't even know her, but I remember that it happened during a swimming period in the morning."

I said, "When we went there, girls and boys didn't use the pool together; a swimming period was for one group or the other. Is that still true?"

"Yes. It was a girls' class. There were a lot of girls in the pool and she must have got a cramp and gone under right away and nobody saw her."

I could rule that one out, I thought, but to keep up my pretense I'd have to show it as much interest as the others.

I asked, "How long was she under? It couldn't have

been more than a minute or two before somebody found her, could it?''

''It probably wasn't, but they couldn't resuscitate her; they tried for a long time. People seem to differ a lot in how they respond to resuscitation; some have been brought back after they've been under water a relatively long time. And with others a minute or two under water is too long.''

''And that leaves the teacher who drowned. You said her name was Bonner?''

''Constance Bonner. That was only four or five months ago, February or March or thereabouts. In this other book, the current one. Do you think I'm silly to keep a journal like this?''

''No, but isn't it a lot of work?''

''Not as much as you'd think. Half an hour or so several times a week. I don't make entries every day, just when something happens worth recording. Pleasant things as well as unpleasant ones. I started doing it five years ago.''

''Too bad,'' I said. ''That means I'm not in it. Unless you put in having lunch with me today.''

Her head was bent over the book in her lap. ''I haven't yet, but maybe I will. I can't seem to find about Constance Bonner.''

''Sure that you made an entry?''

''Yes, almost a page.'' She looked up. ''Sam, that's the only one that might not have been an accident. And if it wasn't, it wouldn't fit your article.''

''You mean she might have been killed deliberately?''

''No, of course not. But there was a strong suspicion that she committed suicide. The circumstances—wait till I find it; I might as well wait to tell you. It's here somewhere.''

Pages turned some more. ''Here it is. It was in January, earlier than I thought. Wait till I read it.''

"Why not read out loud?"

She looked up again. "I'd rather not, Sam. It's just—well, some of the things in these books are so personal that I've never let anyone read a line of it or read any of it to anyone. This particular entry wouldn't matter but—well, it's a matter of principle."

"Okay, I can understand that. Read it to yourself then. Want to kill the rest of that drink so I can make us another?"

"All right. Or are you trying to get me drunk?"

"Deponent refuses to answer," I said.

I heard her close the book while I was making the drinks; out of the corner of my eye I saw her take the three books to a desk in the far corner of the room and lock them into the bottom drawer. She slipped the key in a housecoat pocket and came over to join me at the sink.

"Now that I've read it again, Sam, I think that it *was* suicide. But there wasn't any proof that it was—just circumstances—so the police put it down as accidental, whether they really thought so or not. I mean, they decided she could have fallen in the pool. She couldn't have gone in to swim because she couldn't swim a stroke, and besides she had all her clothes on. But she could have fallen in, except that she had no reason to be there beside the pool."

"It was outside school hours, wasn't it?"

"Yes, it was in the evening. There was an evening meeting of the Drama Club and Miss Bonner was the faculty adviser of the club so naturally she was at the meeting. It was from seven till nine. When the meeting broke up she told the kids she wasn't leaving right away, that she was behind in her work and might as well put in an hour or two in her classroom while she was there, grading papers—it was just after mid-year exams. So when they left, she went to her room—"

"Had she acted normally during the meeting?"

"There were conflicting stories on that from the kids, I remember. Some of them thought she had, others thought she acted strangely. They all agreed that she was pretty quiet and didn't say much, though. Anyway, she walked to the front door with the club members and let them out and locked the door again. She must have gone to her own classroom for at least a while because she turned on the light there although there wasn't anything to indicate that she'd graded any papers.

"Well, about three o'clock in the morning a squad car went by on its regular rounds and the policemen in it saw a light on in the basement of the school and they decided to investigate; sometimes, they knew, teachers worked evenings there, but never until three in the morning. They carried a key to the school, for emergencies, and they let themselves in. They found the light was in a classroom and that a woman's hat and coat were on the desk there, as though she might still be in the building, so they looked around. They kept opening doors and when they opened the one to the room with the pool in it they saw the lights were on in there and they went in. They found her body in the pool."

"That's entirely an inside room," I said. "The lights wouldn't have shown outside. Was Miss Bonner's classroom a basement room?"

"Yes. And not far from the pool. Oh, it *could* have been an accident; she could have gone in there for some reason and fallen in accidentally, and without being able to swim she'd have drowned all right. But why, unless she wanted to commit suicide, would she have gone in there at all?"

"I don't know," I said. "Did they find that she had any reason to kill herself?"

"Well, no specific reason. But her parents—she lived at home with them—said she'd been acting strangely for a few weeks. Happy at times and very unhappy, moping, at other times. Almost—they didn't put it this way—almost manic-depressive. But she wasn't in any trouble that they knew of. I think the police would have called it suicide if they could have found any reason at all for her to have killed herself.''

I said, ''It sounds like suicide to me, Nina. A person's reasons for killing himself wouldn't necessarily show on the surface. Especially if it was true that she was mentally unbalanced. And the symptoms you said her parents described do sound like manic-depressive all right. How well did you know her?''

''Just to speak to. Last year was her first year at South Side, and it just didn't happen that we got acquainted. She was even younger than I by a year or two, about twenty-four, I think. She taught English.''

That one, too, I thought I could forget about. The circumstances just didn't fit, and suicide really seemed like the probable answer. Only two out of the four were left and maybe I was crazy in thinking what I'd been thinking, even about those two.

All right, I thought; I'll quit thinking for tonight.

· 4 ·

I made us another drink. I was feeling mine a little, but I wanted to feel them.

We talked about not much for a while. And then I actually got as far as the door, with my hat on, and Nina with her hand on the knob to open it for me. But I put one arm lightly around her and kissed her. And then both my arms were around her and both hers around me, her hands pressing my head forward, my lips against hers hungrily, so hard that it almost hurt.

After a minute or two I whispered, "I don't want to go, Nina."

"I don't want you to. I know it's wrong, but—"

My lips stopped hers. It seemed right, very right. And I knew now that I'd known all along, since Nina had surprisingly opened the door of Mrs. Chojnacki's flat, that this was going to happen.

It happened very wonderfully, and it still seemed right.

TUESDAY

·1·

I was alone in bed when I awakened. There wasn't a clock in sight and I remembered that Nina was one of those people, she'd told me, who don't need alarm clocks; they make up their minds to awaken at a given hour and always do. My wrist watch told me it was twenty minutes after eight.

I sat up on the edge of the bed and reached for my clothes on the chair beside it. There was a note for me lying on my clothes where I couldn't have missed it.

> Sam: You're still sleeping so soundly that I won't wake you. Get yourself breakfast here if you wish— there'll be coffee left in the pot that you'll only have to heat and you'll find bacon and eggs in the refrigerator—but please be quiet about it. And be quiet when you leave. If you want to phone me during school hours the number is Grand 6400.
>
> Nina

I dressed and left quietly without getting myself breakfast. I didn't know anything about Nina's neighbors, but I didn't want to take a chance of being heard in her apartment at a time when they might know she had already left it. I had breakfast at a restaurant and then drove home. I showered, shaved and put on clean clothes. Then I called Grand 6400. Nina's voice answered.

"Sam, Nina," I said. "Can you talk freely?"

"Yes, sir. He's not in right now. Shall I have him call you back?"

"I'm at home, West 3208. In the phone book, if you didn't write that down. But call as soon as you can—I'll wait here, but I'll just be waiting for your call."

"Yes, sir, I'll have him call you as soon as he comes in. I don't think it will be very long."

It was about ten minutes.

"Sam, I *could* have talked to you, but there were people in the office and I didn't want to have to be careful what I said. I thought I'd rather wait till I could get to the phone booth."

"Give me *some* credit, Nina. You didn't have to explain. Thanks for letting me sleep this morning. I needed it. I feel fine."

"Do you feel the same way you felt last night?"

"Well—at the moment, not exactly. But give me time—until this evening, maybe. You weren't planning anything? For tonight, I mean."

"Not until now."

"Good girl."

"No, I'm not. Would you like me if I was a good girl?"

"Of course not. But listen, darling, I may not be able to see you until late in the evening. There's somebody I've got to see first—and it isn't another woman."

"All right."

"What time will you get home?"

"Before five o'clock, I think. I'm taking off early today, half past one, so I can go to the Chojnacki funeral. After that, if there's time, I'll call on one or two other cases on my list but I'll still be home fairly early."

I said, "I'd forgotten about the funeral. Do you think it will be all right for me to drop in for it?"

"Why—I don't know why you'd want to, but I don't see any reason why you shouldn't."

"Probably see you there, then. 'By, darling."

• 2 •

Chief of Police Steiner was in his office when I got to police headquarters and I had to wait less than half an hour to get in to see him. I handed him a fifty-cent cigar I'd bought on the way there. He peeled off the cellophane and sniffed it appreciatively so I struck while the appreciation held.

"Like you to do me a favor, Chief."

"Always glad to help the *Herald*, Sam." He should be; the *Herald* and Colonel Ackerman had got his job for him. I might have let it go at that, but it would be too easy for him to happen to learn that I was on vacation this week.

I said, "It's for me, not the paper; I'm on my own time. I'm writing a magazine article on accidents—various screwy ways people can get themselves killed. How are chances of my browsing through the file on accidents."

"I guess there's no reason why not. We've got only the non-traffic accidents here, though. If you want the traffic ones—"

"I don't," I said. "Traffic accidents are pretty much all alike, and I'm looking for unusual ones, or ones with screwy angles. Like one I read about recently—forget where it happened but it wasn't here. Painter fell off a platform roped down from the eaves of a building, fell three stories and wasn't hurt a bit except it knocked the wind out of him. Got up and stood there getting his breath back and an unopened can of paint that he'd had on the platform and had knocked over when he fell rolled off the platform three stories above him, hit him on the head and killed him."

Steiner grinned. "Don't recall reading about that one,

but I guess we've had a few funny ones here too. Might remember some if I tried, but if you're going through the files anyway, you'll come across 'em.''

"How's our accident rate compared to other cities?"

"Oh, about in line. If you want statistics on types of accidents and comparison with other cities, look up Carey over in the mayor's office. Year or so ago he did a statistical analysis for the mayor, who wanted to know how we stood compared to other cities. He was mostly interested in traffic accidents, but he covered all kinds while he was at it.''

I didn't see how that would help me but I said thanks, I might do that. Chief Steiner buzzed for his secretary and told him to lead me to the file cabinets on accidents, non-traffic, and turn me loose there.

There was a discouraging number of four-drawer file cabinets. Five of them, all filled with folders on non-traffic accidents. But they didn't look quite so discouraging when the secretary—a tall young man in horn-rimmed glasses—told me they held accident folders for twenty years back, which meant I'd have to go through only a fraction of them.

"There's one drawer for each year," he explained. "The accidents—these are only fatal accidents, of course— are arranged chronologically. But in front of each drawer there's a sheet that's made up at the end of each year, an alphabetical list of names of victims and the date of each, so you can find any given one without having to go through the whole drawer. That is, if you know the name of the victim and the year the accident happened in.''

I told him that was swell. I took off my coat and hung it over a chair and dived in. If the secretary had stuck around to watch me get started I'd have had to carry out my pretext by working chronologically backwards, but he didn't so I started out by looking up, since I knew the year and the names of the victims, the four accidents at South Side High.

Except for addresses, exact dates and times of day, and some irrelevant details, I didn't learn anything beyond what Nina had already told me. I didn't find any mention of the name I was looking for. Not even as a witness.

It was after noon by the time I finished studying those four file folders and I didn't have time, if I was going to have lunch and make the Chojnacki funeral, to start looking through the other files. I talked to the tall secretary again on my way out, explaining that I hadn't finished and would be back later or some other day.

·3·

It was cool and comfortable in Haley's funeral parlor; air-conditioning kept out the heat and the stained-glass windows of the chapel tinted and mellowed the sunlight that came through them.

I sat in a back corner, as inconspicuously as possible. The coffin that held what the roller coaster had left of Jimmy Chojnacki was on a flower-banked bier up at the front.

There were about twenty people there and Nina was the only one I knew. But I could guess that the woman in black next to whom Nina sat and to whom she was whispering must be Anna Chojnacki.

The organ was playing softly now. From outside, far away but getting nearer and louder, came the drone of a plane going overhead. Its sound made me think of the horsefly that had flown around the *Herald* editorial room last Saturday morning and I remembered Harry Rowland's saying, "My God, I thought you were praying."

The minister was praying now and the organ had stopped. He was a tall thin man with a face like a horse,

but with a good voice. I had his name and the name of
his church on the back of an envelope in my pocket.
Haley had told me when I came, thinking that I was
covering the funeral for the paper; not to disillusion him,
I'd written them down.

"For Jesus said, I am the resurrection and the life, in
me shall . . ."

Out of the corner of my eye I saw a man standing
now in the doorway of the chapel, a big man with dark
hair turning gray. The man who was paying for this
funeral, Armin Westphal. I'd wondered if he was going
to come; it was one of my reasons for being here. And
he'd made it, if a little late.

When the prayer was finished he came in quietly and
took the seat nearest the doorway.

The organ played again and a fat Italian-looking woman
with the face of a Madonna sang. Her voice was beautiful. The organist was good, too. He wove little patterns
of notes around the melody, as harpsichord music used
to be written to fill in for the lack of sustained notes.

"In midst of life, we are in death . . ."

I could tell from Anna Chojnacki's shoulders that she
was weeping silently.

I didn't hear the sermon. I was thinking my own
thoughts. Obie Westphal's father had come to the funeral
of Jimmy Chojnacki. Another thing, meaningless in itself
as were all the other things. Why shouldn't he, in a
sudden impulse of generosity caused by relief that his
son was still alive when he'd thought him dead, offer to
pay for the funeral of the boy who'd really died and
whose mother was too poor to pay for it? And why, since
he was paying, shouldn't he come?

But I'd seen Armin Westphal's face last Saturday
afternoon as he'd left here, and I wondered now if this
was the only such funeral he'd paid for.

When the service was over Westphal slipped out

quietly. I gave him time to get away before I left. In case I wanted to talk to him later on some pretext I didn't want him to recognize me as having been at the funeral too.

I wanted more than ever now to have a look at Obie Westphal, in the flesh and not a photograph.

I drove out to the Westphal house. This time I parked beyond it so I wouldn't be in the same place, but I moved my rear vision mirror so I could see all of the front of the house.

I sat there and watched it and nothing happened except that about five o'clock Mr. Westphal came home in the blue Chrysler. This time he put it in the garage instead of leaving it out front. Lights went on inside the house at half past six, and by seven I was beginning to wonder if I was again wasting my time.

There was only one way to find out. I drove to a nearby drugstore and phoned the Westphals. A woman's voice answered and I asked, "Is Obie there?"

"No, he's been visiting a friend in Springfield since Sunday. He'll be back tomorrow at two o'clock. Who shall I tell him called?"

"You needn't bother," I said. "It's nothing important and he wouldn't know my name anyway. I'll call again after he's back."

I hung up and swore at myself for having wasted time both yesterday and today.

I called Nina's number. "This is Sam, darling. Just finished the business I had to do. Have you eaten yet?"

"I was just getting ready to eat. I waited as long as I could and just now gave up hearing from you in time."

"Good, then you can wait a little longer and you'll have a real appetite. Want to grab a cab and meet me somewhere?"

"Let's eat here, Sam, I just took a bath and I'm in my housecoat; I don't feel like getting dressed and going

out. I've got some canned chop suey I can open for us.
How does that sound?''

"Horrible," I said. "I'm feeling carnivorous. If I pick
up a couple of thick steaks will you fry them for us?''

"Will I? That sounds wonderful. I guess I'm feeling
carnivorous too. Hurry, Sam.''

WEDNESDAY

·1·

I woke first. Nina was cuddled against my back and I pulled away, turned and raised myself on one elbow to look at her. Even asleep she was beautiful. Her face was as sweetly innocent as a sleeping baby's. Her hair looked even better a little tousled. She lay with one hand under her chin, her forearm between her breasts, hiding one of them but accentuating the other. I leaned over and kissed it gently.

When I raised up her eyes were open, looking at me.

"Love me, Sam?"

"I don't know," I said honestly. "I was just wondering. I know I want you." I lay down again and pulled her tightly against me.

"You shouldn't love me," she said. "You mustn't."

"Why not?"

"I'm a wicked woman."

"Prove it."

She nibbled gently at my ear. I said, "That's not very wicked."

"What do you want me to do? *This?*"

· 2 ·

Again I went home to clean up and change. At ten o'clock, which I figured was late enough, I drove to Radnik Street and parked in front of the tenement in which Mrs. Chojnacki lived. I sat in the car a minute or two thinking up what approach I should use in talking to her. I could, of course, get her to talk freely by introducing myself as a friend of Nina's, but I didn't want to do that; she'd tell Nina I'd been there and then I'd have to explain to Nina and that wouldn't be easy without telling her the whole story. And I wasn't telling anyone that, as long as I had so little to back it up.

So I had to work out a lie, and I decided against using even my right name lest, in talking to Nina later, Jimmy's mother might mention it.

I went up the stairs and knocked on the door and this time Nina didn't open it. I'd seen Mrs. Chojnacki at the funeral service but not closely. She was tall and thin, almost gaunt, and with huge tragic eyes.

I said, "My name is Herbert Johnson, Mrs. Chojnacki. I'm an attorney." She looked a little blank. "A lawyer. I represent the person who paid for your son's funeral. He would like to know—"

"You come in."

I went in. The room and the furniture were shabby, but clean and neat.

"You sit down, Mr. Johnson. You like cup coffee maybe?"

I started to decline, then realized that drinking coffee would keep me there long enough to work the conversation any way I wanted it to go, and to do it casually. So I said yes, I'd like coffee. She went into the kitchen and came back in a few minutes.

"Is making. You from man who runs ride at the park?"

"I'm sorry," I told her, "my client wants to remain anony—he doesn't want anybody to know who he is. What we want to know is whether the service Mr. Haley gave you was satisfactory. Before we pay the bill, in other words, we want to be sure everything was all right."

"Yes, *very* nice funeral. I saw you there."

I nodded. "My employer wasn't able to come, so I came instead."

"Thank you. Thank you much."

"My employer said to tell you that paying for the funeral isn't much, but he's glad he was able to do that for you."

"You thank him for me. Was very kind."

I said, "I can't tell you how sorry I am about Jimmy, Mrs. Chojnacki. Personally, I mean. I've heard a lot about him. He must have been a fine boy."

"Good boy, yes. Sometimes he was bad but— He died good. I thank God for that."

"He went to South Side High School, didn't he?"

"For one year, yes. Then—"

I spoke quickly to save her embarrassment. "I know a boy who goes there; he must have been in Jimmy's class. Obie Westphal, Henry O. Westphal his right name is. Did your Jimmy know him, do you happen to know?"

"He never say name. I don't know. I don't know all his friends, so could be he knew that boy you say."

"Who was Jimmy's closest friend?"

"Pete Brenner. All the time with Pete Brenner. Other friends, sometimes, mostly Pete."

"Is Pete Brenner going to South Side now?"

"No, he quit after two years, to work. In fruit market down block. Wait, I get coffee now."

I waited, and filled in the time looking around to find a picture that might be Jimmy Chojnacki. I couldn't find one. So when Mrs. Chojnacki came back with coffee for both of us, I got her talking about her son. She talked readily, seemed to want to talk about him. What wasn't irrelevant, though, was stuff I'd already learned from Nina. But I let myself seem to get more and more interested until when I asked if she had a photograph of him I could see, the question seemed natural.

"Yes, *good* picture. Last year man came selling coupons for picture, only dollar. But cost six dollars more after. You want to see, Mr. Johnson?"

I wanted to see. She went into the bedroom and came back with a four-by-six portrait photo in a cardboard folder and handed it to me.

Jimmy Chojnacki had been a good-looking boy. His face was a bit weak, but not vicious. And he had those deep-set, dreamy eyes some Polish kids have. And behind the dreaminess a sort of Gypsy wildness. Looking at that picture it no longer seemed quite so strange that he'd been both a pickpocket and an embryonic writer. A dreamer and a thief. Well, François Villon had combined those qualities and had done a good job of it. Maybe Jimmy Chojnacki would have, too. If he'd had a chance.

I admired the picture and said I thought my employer would like to see it or a copy of it, that he'd never seen Jimmy and would be interested. Would she mind if I borrowed the picture just long enough for me to let a photographer copy it? Or did she have the negative that she could lend me instead?

I got a break; she had extra copies of the picture and I could have one; she was glad to send one to the man who paid for Jimmy's funeral. She'd been high-pressured, I gathered, into taking half a dozen prints besides the one covered by her coupon and still had two of them left besides the one in my hand so I could have that one to take with me. I put it in my pocket and thanked her.

I managed to find out one thing more by leading the conversation around to Whitewater Beach and how often Jimmy had gone there. He went there often, almost every Saturday. And last Saturday, as far as she knew, he'd gone there alone.

I drove downtown. Now that I had a picture of the Chojnacki boy I needed a picture of Obie. And there was a good one in the *Herald* morgue.

The morgue is on the second floor, the editorial offices on the third. If I used the back stairs I probably wouldn't see anyone I knew except old Hackenschmidt, who ran the morgue, and he probably wouldn't know I was on vacation this week. He didn't, and I got the picture without question, and I didn't see anyone to whom I had to explain what I was doing there when I was supposed to be fishing at Laflamme.

I drove south again and put my car in the parking lot at Whitewater Beach. It was almost noon then; most of the concessions would be open, even on a weekday.

I walked slowly down the midway. Most of the smaller concessions were open, the ones that would probably have been open as early as ten last Saturday. None of them was doing much business as yet. The few that had people in front of them at the moment I skipped and went back to after I'd talked to the concessionaires at places beyond. I showed each of them the two photographs, one of Jimmy and one of Obie. All I wanted to know was whether they remembered seeing the two boys together or either of them separately. When I got an affirmative answer I tried to pin it down as to when.

But I didn't get any affirmative answer concerning seeing the two boys together. A lot of them remembered seeing Jimmy around. No special times, just around in general. Which wasn't surprising, since I already knew he'd hung around the park a lot. The girl on duty at the lemonade stand said he'd bought drinks there quite a few times, she thought. But she didn't remember when the last time was, except that she didn't recall seeing him for a week or two. And Obie's picture drew a complete blank from her. He'd looked vaguely familiar to a few others. Only one person—a ring game concessionaire— definitely recognized him, and it turned out that he didn't remember seeing him at the park; he was a football fan who followed high school football and had seen Obie play. He was only a few years out of high school and had played football himself. He wanted to talk football but I didn't want to. I moved on. The first time up the midway I had to skip the lunch stand that was almost across the areaway that led back to the first dip of the Blue Streak; it was too busy.

On my way back, picking up the few I'd missed the first time, I took the Blue Streak for a stopover because my beefy friend in the sailor straw had just got there. He wasn't operating yet, but he was doing some paper work in the ticket booth. I rapped on the glass and he raised the window.

"Hi," I said. "Recognize either of these kids?"

He looked at the pictures I put on the ledge in front of him and then shook his head.

"You saw one of them all right," I told him.

He looked puzzled for a second. "You mean one of 'em's the kid who—"

"I thought you were the first one there. Didn't you see him?"

"Jesus, did I see him? Face down across the tracks I saw him. And I didn't roll him over to look at his face either. Why should I?" He looked down again at the pictures. "But if it's one of these, it'd have to be the dark-haired one, not the blond kid. Say, are you still harping on that accident? I thought you was writing an article on roller coasters.''

"I am. But there's one angle on the accident I'm still investigating. Probably doesn't mean anything.''

"On the level, you a reporter? Or a cop?''

"A reporter.'' I grinned at him. "Which means I could be either one. I mean, if I was a cop I could say I was a reporter. But if I was a reporter I couldn't claim to be a cop—not without going to jail for it.''

I left him puzzling that out and went on down the midway. The lunch stand still had customers. But it occurred to me that I was getting hungry myself so I stopped and ordered a hamburger sandwich. When the grizzled man who ran the counter brought it to me a few minutes later I had the two pictures lying on the counter facing him. "Recognize either of these kids?'' I asked him.

He bent over to look at the pictures. "Umm—that dark-haired kid I've seen around. And the blond one too, but not so often.''

"Ever see them together?''

"Don't think so.''

"Remember when you last saw the blond one?''

"Hell, no. I see thousands of people a day. How'd I remember— Hey, wait a minute.''

He rescued two hamburgers off the grill and put them into buns and served them. Then he came back.

"Look,'' he said. "I might remember at that. But why should I? I might be getting the kid in trouble. You a cop?''

I said, "I'm a lawyer. And you might be getting the kid *out* of trouble. He's in it already, and he needs an alibi for—for a certain time. He says he was here at the park then and I'm trying to find somebody who can prove he was.''

"When's the time?''

"Wouldn't mean much if I told you first, would it?"

"It was Saturday morning, early."

"How early? Before ten o'clock?"

"Damn if I know. I got here around past nine, maybe a little later, but I was busy for a while getting things ready. He was my first customer that day. It could have been before ten."

"How do you remember for sure it was last Saturday?"

"That was the day the kid was killed on the Blue Streak. Jeez, I heard it—heard wood splintering and the noise the car made when it ran off—and ran over there."

"Was that before or after the blond kid bought something here?"

"After. But it couldn't have been more'n a few minutes after."

"But he wasn't still eating at the counter?"

"No. I'm sure because I took a look to be sure there weren't any customers, or any coming. Then I pulled the bills out of the register—took a chance on the change—and ran over to see what the crash had been."

"Did you see the blond kid over there?"

"Not that I remember. There were six or seven people around by the time I got there, but I don't remember him being one of them."

"You're sure he was alone while he was at the counter here?"

"Sure. He bought a coke, that's all, and stood there to drink it. The bottle was on the counter."

"Did you see him leave? Which way he walked?"

"Nope, I was back getting things ready for the day's business. I didn't stand there *watching* him drink the coke and go away. All I know is he wasn't there any more by the time I heard the crash."

And that was all I was going to learn from him, so I followed through with my pretense of wanting an alibi witness by taking down his name and home address. And

I'd finished my hamburger by then and wandered off. I tried the couple of remaining concessions I hadn't got yet and then went to the parking lot and got in my car.

I hadn't really expected to, but I'd got something after all. Not much, but something. Obie had been right near the scene of the accident and just before it had happened. If only I could have found someone who'd seen him and Jimmy *together* just before the accident . . .

What do you mean, accident? I asked myself.

And not murder either, exactly. Murder means there's a motive. And Obie had no motive for killing Jimmy Chojnacki. Certainly and above all, he didn't know that his billfold was in Jimmy's pocket.

But does a tiger need a motive? Oh, it has one often: hunger. But not always even that. A rogue tiger will kill for the pure savage joy of killing.

· 3 ·

I had a date with a tiger.

Not to talk to, not yet, but damn it I wanted a look at him. And I was pretty sure I could see him at the railroad station at two o'clock. Mrs. Westphal had said he'd be back "at two o'clock" from Springfield and there was a two o'clock train that came through there. If he'd been coming back by car she'd have said "early in the afternoon" rather than such a specific hour. Private automobiles don't follow timetables.

It was now half past twelve; I didn't want to eat lunch yet, though, because the hamburger had killed my appetite. And it was too soon to start for the railroad station.

Maybe, while I was so near, I could look up the Pete Brenner whom Mrs. Chojnacki had mentioned as Jimmy's best friend. She'd said he worked at the fruit market "down the block"; there wouldn't be more than one or two fruit markets on Radnik Street in or near the 2900 block. And it would kill time for me.

I drove to Radnik and along it slowly. There was a fruit market near Paducah, a block and a half from where Mrs. Chojnacki lived. I found a place to park and went inside.

It was fairly busy. There were more customers than clerks so no clerk accosted me, and none of them was a kid that could have been Pete Brenner. I walked on to an open doorway at the back and looked through. A boy of about seventeen was working at a big table back there, bunching carrots. The color of his hair just matched the carrots he was handling. I went through the doorway and walked up to him.

"You're Pete Brenner?" I asked him.

He turned around and his eyes gave me a dusting-over. They weren't shifty eyes, but they were hard and suspicious. They took all of me in before he said "Yeah."

He was going to be tough to handle. He wasn't going to swallow any of the stories I'd been handing around so glibly the last few days. He wasn't going to answer any questions beyond that first one without having a reason to answer them.

There was only one reason I could give him, besides the truth and I wasn't going to give him that. I took the reason out of my billfold. "Want to earn a fin by answering a few questions?"

"Who are you?"

I grinned at him. "If I'm answering the questions it'll cost you a fin instead of me."

"What are the questions?"

"They're about Jimmy Chojnacki. And he's dead so you can't do him any harm by answering them."

He looked up over my shoulder at what must have

been a clock on the wall behind me. He said, "I'm takin' off for lunch in four minutes. Wait outside. Boss don't like me to gab in here while I'm workin'."

"Okay, Pete," I said. I went through the fruit store again and waited just outside the door.

In a few minutes he came out. He said, "I got only a half hour. Can we talk while I eat?"

"If it's near here."

"Across the street. That hamburger place."

I thought I could eat another hamburger myself by now. Added to the one I'd eaten at the park it would hold me until dinner time. "Swell," I said.

We sat at the counter, down at the far end. I took out the five-dollar bill and put it down between us as soon as the counterman had taken our orders and had gone front to the grill. Pete Brenner glanced at it but didn't make any move to pick it up.

He said, "Listen, you can't buy me for five bucks. Besides that, I want to know who you are and what this is all about. If it's okay, then I'll answer your questions— if I like 'em."

No, there wasn't going to be any use handing him a story I couldn't prove. He was a tough little redhead, and he knew it.

I put my press pass on the counter. I said, "I'm a reporter. There's my name and my paper, the *Herald*. I think I've got an angle on Jimmy's accident. Maybe it's screwy but if it isn't, it's going to be a big story. And it can't hurt Jimmy. If I get the story I won't quote you unless you want me to, so it can't hurt you."

"What's the angle?"

"That's my business. I'd be a sucker to tell you. You could take it to a reporter on the other paper in town and peddle it to him."

"Let's see if I like the questions."

"You were Jimmy Chojnacki's closest friend?"

"I guess I was."

"When did you last see him?"

"The evening before he was killed, up to about midnight. Him and me bummed around awhile, shot some pool. He was goin' home when he left me."

"Did he say anything about what he was going to do the next day, Saturday?"

"Yeah, he said he'd probably go over to the park, Whitewater."

"Alone?"

"I guess so. I usta go with him sometimes but since I got this fruit market job I can't get off Saturdays. That's the busiest day they got there."

"You're sure he wasn't going to meet anyone there?"

"Hell no, I'm not sure. But if he was he didn't say so to me."

The counterman was bringing our sandwiches. "Which one of you wanted the French fries with?"

"Mine's the plain one," I said.

He reached for the five on the counter. "Take 'em both out of this?"

"Sure."

He brought the change and left. I pocketed it and put down another five-dollar bill.

Pete looked at it. "That's all you wanted to know?"

I nodded, and he stuck the bill into his pocket. "You didn't get much for it," he said.

"Guess I didn't," I said. I hadn't, but then I hadn't expected much. And I hadn't yet asked the final question; I'd waited deliberately until after he'd taken the money so I could ask it casually. I was pretty sure he'd answer anyway, and it wouldn't be one of the paid-for answers.

I waited some more, until we'd almost finished our sandwiches and until a few remarks about how damn hot the weather had been had intervened. Then I asked, "Do you know a boy named Obie Westphal?"

"Sure. That is I know him by sight; I don't really *know* him. He was in my class at high. I mean, the class I was in until I quit a year ago."

"Do you know if Jimmy knew him?"

"Just about like I did, I guess."

"He never mentioned him?"

"Not unless we happened to be talking about football. We both went to a couple of South Side games last fall so naturally we talked about 'em. But Jimmy didn't really *know* Obie, or maybe just enough to say hi."

He picked up the last of his French fries and then turned to look at me before he put it in his mouth. "What's Obie got to do with this?"

"Nothing," I said. "I went to South Side myself and still see a football game now and then. I was trying to remember whether Obie would be playing this coming season or whether he graduated last June."

"Oh. Well, he's got a year to go. He started as a freshman the year Jimmy and me started, so he was a junior last year." His eyes turned hard and suspicious again. "How'd you know we went to South Side? I didn't say that till after you asked about Obie?"

"You're not the first person I talked to. How'd you think I knew you were a friend of Jimmy's, and found you?"

"All right, how did you?"

"That'll cost *you* five dollars."

He laughed. "You win. Thanks for the fin, and the lunch."

I left him in front of the restaurant and walked to my car. I'd have to drive fairly fast now to make the railroad station by two o'clock.

·4·

I made it, and I needn't have hurried. The bulletin board showed that the train was going to be twenty minutes late. The station was crowded, and it was hot as hell. I couldn't find a vacant seat, so I leaned against a post that gave me a good view of the door he'd come through.

I watched the door and waited.

I knew him the minute he came through it. He looked a bit older than he looked on the picture in my pocket and quite a bit bigger than I'd guessed him to be. Quite a bit bigger than I am. At least six feet tall and a hundred and eighty, maybe ninety pounds. He was a young giant with shoulders made to order for football. He had short blond hair and didn't wear a hat. He was good-looking as hell. Just about every girl who saw him would be nuts about him.

He carried a light suitcase—at least it seemed light the way he carried it, but from the look of his shoulders he might have carried it that way even if it had been loaded with bricks. He put it down just inside the door and stood looking around. Then he grinned; he yelled "Hi, guys!" He picked up the suitcase and started toward two other young men—or high school kids, whichever you want to call them—about his age. Both of them wore striped T shirts; one of them carried what looked like a clarinet case.

They stood talking a minute and then all three drifted over to the soft drink counter. They had cokes and Obie paid for them. He drank two himself, rapidly, as though the train ride had made him thirsty. Then the three of them headed for the door labeled *Men* and went through it.

I found a vacant seat on a bench from which I could watch the door without being conspicuous. I watched it for what seemed quite a while, and when I looked at my watch I saw that it had been quite a while. I remembered then that the men's room of the railroad station had a door on the other side that led through a cigar store to the street.

I went into the men's room and they weren't there. I went on into the cigar store and they weren't there, either; not that I'd expected them to be. I thought, what a hell of a shadow I'd make.

The proprietor was picking his teeth behind the cigar counter. I bought a cigar and asked, "Three high school kids come through here from the station a few minutes ago? One of 'em a big blond kid?"

"Yeah," he said. He took the toothpick out of his mouth. "They got in that car that's been parked out front, the one I been laughing at."

"What about it?

"Stripped-down jalopy with a wolf's head on the radiator cap and painted on the side, *'Don't laugh; your daughter may be inside.'* "

"The blond kid drive it?"

"Nope, the one with the squealer."

"Squealer?"

"The clary, the licorice stick." He grinned. "I talk the language. I got two kids in high."

"God help you," I said. "Have a cigar."

I gave him back the cigar I'd just bought from him and went out, leaving him staring at me.

I got in my own car half a block down the street and sat there trying to think until I realized how hot I was and that I could think just as well with the car moving, no matter where.

That is, if I could think at all. Just then, I could only
wonder if I was stark raving mad to have thought *what*
I'd thought about Obie Westphal. Now that I'd actually
seen him it didn't really seem possible. Tigers drink
blood, not cokes. And one may smile and be a villain,
but can a homicidal maniac grin as Obie had grinned at
his friends? I didn't know.

I was driving toward South Side High School, I realized, and only a few blocks away now. And then I was
in front of it and I swung the Buick in to the curb and
cut the engine. I sat there looking at my alma mater, at
the big beautiful building set well back from the street.
A proud building and a building to be proud of, with a
proud straight tower that went three stories higher than
the rest of the building. And it would have been from
one of those three windows in the middle floor of the
tower, five stories above the concrete steps, that the
freshman named Wilbur Greenough had fallen—or had
been pushed. The year Obie had entered high school.

But did that mean anything? Do two and two make
twenty-two?

I suddenly realized that I was parked in plain sight of
the windows of the school office and that if Nina should
look out she might see and recognize the car and wonder
why I was parking there.

I started the engine again and drove away. I headed
for the Westphal house. I wanted to think things out and
if I parked where I could watch the house again—this
time knowing at least that Obie was in town—I'd have
plenty of chance to think while I did my watching.

I parked again where I'd parked the first time I'd been
there; it was the better of the two places to park by day
because my car was under a big oak that shaded it.

A man in work clothes, a handyman or a part-time
gardener no doubt, was mowing the lawn behind the
white picket fence. He stopped often to take off his hat

and wipe sweat off his face and forehead with a big blue bandanna. The whirring of the lawnmower was a familiar, homey sound.

Let's start, I thought, with Jimmy Chojnacki. Why was I sure that Jimmy's death hadn't been an accident?

Lots of little things. Mainly the sound of the ratchet on the first uphill of the roller coaster. It's a sound that's too loud to be overlooked and it's unmistakable for what it is. From the bottom of the hill beyond that first upgrade no one could possibly not hear it and not know that a car was coming. Only someone deliberately trying to commit suicide would choose that time to cross the tracks.

Well, people *do* commit suicide. Why couldn't Jimmy have lain down across the tracks and waited for the car to kill him?

Because people don't commit suicide suddenly and irrelevantly in the middle of another act. I suppose a pickpocket may decide to kill himself, as anyone else might, but it wouldn't be in the middle of an act of crime, a freshly lifted billfold in his pocket. Even if, after stealing Obie's wallet, Jimmy had decided to kill himself, automatic reflexes would have seen him complete the act of theft by taking the money out of the wallet and getting rid of the leather. I happened to know a pickpocket once during my days as a police reporter. I'd talked over his profession with him—he was proud of his skill and liked to talk about it—he told me that a pickpocket's first and obsessive thought, once he's lifted a wallet, is to get the incriminating evidence of the wallet itself off his person as quickly as possible. And there are plenty of ways of getting rid of one unobserved, even in a crowd; he'd told me some of the most common methods. And if Jimmy had been back there by the roller coaster tracks alone, he could have got rid of it easily. Even if he'd thrown it away without bothering to take the money out of it, he wouldn't have killed himself with it in his pocket. He'd surely have thought of his mother, if for no other reason, and he couldn't have known that the police would not tell her that he had died with stolen property in his pocket.

Nor is suicide itself, I believe, ever a sudden and unpremeditated thing. It's an idea that takes build-up, working up one's courage to the irrevocable act. And while a man—or an adolescent boy—is building up his courage to match his despair he most certainly would not take time out to pick a pocket on his way to death.

No, suicide was out completely, much, much less likely than accident.

There was even, come to think of it, one way in which it could have been an accident.

Jimmy could have seen Obie drinking his coke at the stand. Possibly Obie had paid for it with a bill out of his wallet and Jimmy had seen the wallet and the pocket into which Obie had returned it. Jimmy could have walked behind Obie, lifted the wallet, headed quickly for the low fence that led back to privacy. Obie could have turned and seen Jimmy walking away rapidly—he'd have been too smart to run—and, remembering why Jimmy had been expelled from school, could have touched his wallet pocket and found the wallet gone. He could have given chase and Jimmy, running for his freedom, might in that case have taken the chance of trying to beat the descending car across the tracks, tripped and fallen. . . .

That's a way it *could* have happened as an accident. But if so, why would Obie have ducked instead of staying and explaining what had happened?

And why had Obie's father not looked happy to learn that his son was still alive, and why had he offered to pay for the funeral of the boy who'd died in Obie's stead?

It could be reconstructed another way and those things would be explained.

Obie had turned and had seen Jimmy heading for the

fence, but did *not*, as yet, miss his wallet. He had waved and said "Hi" and Jimmy would, of course, have stopped. Obie, his coke finished, had strolled over and asked Jimmy where he'd been going back there. Jimmy, frightened because he had Obie's wallet, would have . . .

I tried to put myself in Jimmy's place. What would I have said? "Just going to take a look around back there." And Obie, "What's back there?"

I'd have figured, if I'd been Jimmy, that the wallet, now that Obie'd seen me, was too hot to keep. But back there I could drop it, money and all, the first chance I had. And when Obie missed it I'd help him hunt for it and find it for him if he didn't find it himself. The money would still be in it and although Obie might suspect what had really happened there wouldn't be any proof that it hadn't simply fallen out of his pocket. He wouldn't do anything about it.

Back by the tracks, the wallet still in Jimmy's pocket. Burning him, but he'd have to wait for a moment when Obie was walking ahead before he would dare take it out and drop it.

The clicking of the ratchet. The roller coaster car coming up the hill. Neither of them would have to explain to the other what that sound was. Obie saying "Let's stand here and watch it come down past us." Side by side, possibly three feet back from the tracks. The car coming over the top of the hill—empty, no witnesses. Obie taking a quick look back to be sure nobody happens to be standing on the midway, looking back toward them, in the one small area that afforded a view back over the fence. Nobody. They are completely unobserved. His hand going up behind Jimmy Chojnacki's back and, just as the car roars toward the bottom of the hill . . .

Then, quickly, over the outer fence only a few yards beyond the tracks. Out of sight he could have been, almost before the crash had quit echoing. Thinking, once he was clear, that there was nothing at all to connect him with Jimmy Chojnacki—until, later, he discovered that his wallet was gone and maybe guessed what had happened to it. But having to go back anyway to inquire at the Lost and Found Department. Learning that the wallet had caused an erroneous preliminary identification, that his parents were coming back.

And did Obie know that his father would guess the truth?

A car drove past mine and swung in to the curb in front of the Westphal house, brakes squealing with the suddenness of the stop. Well, technically it was a car. It had four wheels and a body. But there weren't any fenders over the wheels and there wasn't a top over the body, not even a folded-back one. There was a moth-eaten wolf's head where the radiator cap should have been and there was lettering on the side of the body; it had gone past too fast for me to read and the angle was wrong now, but the cigar-store proprietor had already told me what the lettering was.

There were seven in it now, all of high school age, four boys and three girls. The boy who'd carried the clarinet case was behind the wheel, and a girl and Obie in the front seat with him; the other four, two and two, were in the back seat. Obie got out, waved and said something I couldn't hear, and went through the gate and up to the house. He was still carrying his suitcase so apparently they'd been riding around—and getting recruits—since I'd seen three of them at the station. The jalopy started off so fast that I think the back wheels spun before they gripped the pavement.

I remembered that detectives in stories always carefully time the observed movements of a suspect, so I looked at my watch. It was twenty-seven minutes after four o'clock, if that matters.

I could hear the slam of the screen door as he went inside.

I went back to my thinking. I'd thought of the four fatal accidents at South Side High within three years the moment I'd begun to suspect that there was something not kosher about Jimmy Chojnacki's death. Maybe just the fact that both Jimmy and Obie had gone to South Side made me think of them. I had to admit that they didn't look very conclusive now. One of them was definitely eliminated; he could hardly have killed the girl who'd drowned in the girls' swimming class. And the drowning of the teacher seemed pretty unlikely. It didn't fit the pattern of the others. But there was one thing I wanted to know: Had Obie been a member of the Drama Club? Was he one of the group Miss Bonner had let out of the building after the meeting that night, so he could have known she was going to be there alone that night? If he had been, then I still couldn't rule out Constance Bonner as at least a possibility. I'd have to remember, next time I was with Nina, to lead the conversation around to Obie so I could ask whether she happened to know if he belonged to the Drama Club. No, I couldn't ask it just that way; I'd have to ask if she knew what school activities if any Obie went in for besides athletics. That would be a natural enough question.

Or where could I look at a last year's Year Book of the high school? It would have a group photograph of the Drama Club and I could see whether Obie was on it.

A few minutes before five o'clock Mr. Westphal came home in the Chrysler. Again he put it away in the garage.

At six o'clock it occurred to me that since Obie was still home he was obviously going to stay there at least through dinner, even if he was going out somewhere in the evening. And that now would be a good time for me to dash away for something to eat and I'd have time to get back before he left if he was going to leave. I drove to a restaurant and had a quick meal. I got back not much after six-thirty, and felt pretty sure he'd hardly have left sooner than that. He hadn't; he obligingly proved it at

seven o'clock by coming out on the porch for a few
minutes, apparently for a little fresh air. He didn't glance
toward my car; it was getting fairly dark by then, though,
and I doubt if he could have seen that anyone was sitting
in the car even if he had looked. I was sure it was Obie
and not his father only because he strolled to the end of
the porch and back and I saw him briefly silhouetted
twice against a lighted window.

After he went back in I began to feel that I was wasting
my time. He probably wouldn't go anywhere, his first
night back home after his trip to Springfield. And if he
did and I followed him, he'd probably go only to a movie
or a friend's house.

Well, what did I expect him to do? Go hunting?

· 5 ·

At nine o'clock he went hunting.

He came out and stood on the porch a minute. I thought
maybe it was for another breath of fresh air and I was
going to call it a night if he went back in.

But he came on down the steps and out the gate in
the white picket fence. He turned west and started walking, not fast, not slow. He passed my car, but on his
own side of the street; he didn't look my way. It was
plenty dark by then and he couldn't possibly have seen
that anyone was in the car if he had looked.

I waited until he'd gone almost a block before I got
out of the car and started to walk after him. I kept on
my side of the street and kept my distance. The streets
were almost deserted and I didn't dare get closer. There
were trees and I couldn't see him often, but I'd get an
occasional glimpse.

We weren't heading toward any bright-light district. We weren't heading anywhere that I knew of unless it could be the freight yards, the jungles.

When he turned at the next corner I knew that's where we were going. We were on a street now, after I'd made the turn too, where there weren't any trees to give me cover, but I took a chance and closed up the distance a little anyway. I was less than half a block behind him when he started across the first tracks.

But it didn't do any good; I lost him completely the minute he got in among the cars. It's a fairly big jungle; dozens of tracks wide and almost a mile long. A hundred people could lose themselves in it.

I wandered around for half an hour and then gave up. I didn't even see any hoboes; there were probably some around but they'd be asleep in empty boxcars by now probably.

I went back the way we'd come and got in my car and sat there. A little after half past ten Obie came walking back. He went inside the house and a couple of minutes later I saw a light go on in an upstairs front room and saw Obie's silhouette against the shade; he was going to bed.

I drove to the nearest tavern and had myself a drink. While the bartender was pouring me a second one I went to the phone booth at the back. I dialed a number and got an answer.

"This is Sam, Nina. May I come around?"

"Why—I thought you weren't coming tonight, Sam. I'm in bed."

"Wonderful," I said. "I'll be with you in twenty minutes."

THURSDAY

· 1 ·

People should never talk at breakfast. Not about anything serious, anyway. At breakfast one is too sensible, one sees things too clearly on the practical side.

Nina and I got up at the same time and she'd insisted on making breakfast for both of us.

She started it. "Sam, if you don't mind my asking, what were you doing yesterday evening? I know it's none of my business but—"

It wasn't, but I could hardly tell her that. I should have had a lie ready but I didn't have, and I couldn't think of one on such short notice.

"Working," I said.

"But isn't this your vacation?"

"Sure. This was research for something I'm free-lancing. It wouldn't interest you."

"How do you know it wouldn't? Of course, if you want to be mysterious about it—"

"Nina," I said, "you're talking just like a wife."

I know I couldn't have found a worse thing to say if I'd worked on it. I looked up at her to see how she'd taken it, and she hadn't. She was glaring at me.

"I'm sorry," I said. "I shouldn't have said that. I didn't mean it. And I didn't mean to sound mysterious; I just didn't want to sound boring. I'm still working on that article about buildings being accident-prone. Yesterday afternoon I spent at police headquarters going through their accident records and statistics. Yesterday evening I spent at the *Journal*, hunting up things in the morgue.''

"The *Journal*? Why not your own paper?"

"It's an afternoon paper. The *Journal*'s a morning one. There's a skeleton force on evenings in some departments, at the *Herald*, but the morgue isn't open. And I've got friends at the *Journal* who fixed it for me to use their morgue.'' I grinned at her. "From what happened afterward, at least you can't suspect me of spending the evening consorting with another woman.''

It should have made her smile but it didn't. She said, "It wouldn't have been any business of mine if you had, Sam. This is just—just an affair between us. I haven't any claim on you.''

Why must women always bring up things like that? It was perfectly true, of course. Particularly from Nina's point of view because she hadn't known there was a possibility of its being anything more. I'd told her that Millie was out of town for a week or so, nothing beyond that. I didn't think it was fair to tell Nina that there was a possibility of Millie and me breaking up our marriage. I hadn't seduced Nina by holding out a possibility of marrying her. Time enough to tell her about that if and when it happened and if, by then, I was sure I wanted to marry her. I thought I was sure, but—well, there's a big difference between wanting like hell to sleep with a woman and wanting to marry her.

But how the hell could I answer what she'd just said.

I tried. "Nina, what we're having is something wonderful. And it's not just physical; you know that. I don't know whether there's love involved—partly because I'm not sure what love is—but there's at least affection. Affection and enjoyment—isn't that enough to go on, for a while anyway?"

But this seemed to be her morning for soul-probing.

"Sam, do you think I'm a p-pushover? You must think so."

I could laugh at that. "No man's ego, darling, will ever let him think a woman is a pushover for other men just because *he* can have her."

No, no man's ego ever lets him *think* that, but he always wonders a little.

I could see from her face, though, that the answer didn't completely satisfy her so I did what I should have done several minutes ago. I walked around the breakfast table, put my arms around her, bent down and kissed her. That's the only answer that makes sense to such questions as she'd been asking. Women always twist the meaning of words but they can't twist the meaning of a kiss—and they understand it better, anyway.

We finished breakfast in peace.

And I had sense enough to walk to the door with her— again she wanted me to wait a few minutes after she'd left so we wouldn't be seen leaving together—and put my arms around her and kiss her again.

But after the kiss she said, "Sam—" And I said, "Yes, darling?"

"I don't think you'd better come around—or even phone—tonight."

"Why not?"

"Well—if for no other reason, I need *sleep*. At least one good *long* night's sleep. I want to get to bed by nine o'clock—and to sleep. I'm a working girl, Sam."

"All right," I said. "Eliminate the 'if for no other reason' and it's a deal."

"Fine. I *do* need sleep, Sam. I guess that's why I'm irritable. I guess there isn't any other reason."

I kissed her again and this time she kissed back as though she meant it.

• 2 •

I went back to the salt mines. I hadn't mined any salt the other time I'd been there but then I'd taken time to look only at the file folders on the four fatal accidents at the high school. This time I wanted to do some random and miscellaneous browsing through as many of the other files as I could cover in a day.

But first I wanted to eliminate a possibility. Before I went to the file cabinets I stopped by the desk of the male clerk to whom I'd talked day before yesterday.

"Heard there was an accident in the jungles last night. Have you had a report on it yet?"

"The jungles? Oh, you mean the freight yards. No, there wasn't any last night."

"Sure you'd have the report by now?"

"Oh, yes. It would have been on my desk this morning. There were reports on four accidents last night, one of them a fatality, but they were all auto accidents."

"I thought they weren't handled in this department."

"They aren't. Traffic department, upstairs, handles them. But we get a duplicate of the preliminary report on any accident that involves car damage or bodily injury. Chief Steiner likes to look them all over, just in case."

I said, "I don't get it. In case of what?"

"In case one of them might correlate with something else we're working on. Say there's a robbery somewhere at two o'clock in the morning, two men involved. And it turns out there was a traffic accident, two men in a speeding car, several miles away and twenty minutes later. Might or might not be the same two men, but it'd be worth checking. It takes only a minute or two a day for him to give the traffic accident reports a quick look and once in a while it pays off. Ever hear of Tony Colletti?''

"Sure, the bank robber. He was caught here a few years ago.''

"Because the Chief read accident reports. We'd had a tip that Colletti was in this neck of the woods and one morning there was a report on a minor accident involving a guy named Anthony Cole. Antonio Coletti—Anthony Cole. And an out-of-state license and driver's license. Where'd you hear there was an accident in the freight yards last night?''

"Just an overheard conversation in a tavern,'' I said. "I must have heard wrong about when it happened. But I'd like to check through past accidents that may have happened there. Do you have a cross index to them, by any chance, or will I just have to come across them in the files?''

"If they're accidents involving moving vehicles—which includes freight engines or freight cars if they're moving at the time—you'll find them upstairs in traffic. It's a funny technicality maybe but we've got to draw the line between traffic and non-traffic accidents somewhere and that's the line.''

"You mean if a hobo falls off a stationary boxcar it's a non-traffic accident, but if he falls off one while it's moving—even being shunted around a freight yard, it's a traffic accident?''

"Sounds screwy but that's the way it is. Of course most railroad accidents are outside freight yards and really are traffic accidents.''

"Thanks,'' I said. "Think before I start on these files I'll mosey upstairs and see if they have a separate file on freight-yard accidents. I've got a hunch I'll find some

I can use. Will I have to get permission from somebody to look at the files up there?"

"Don't see why. The Chief said to let you look through the accident files and those are accident files too. But ask them to phone down and check with me—my name's Springer—if they give you any trouble."

They didn't give me any trouble.

Better yet, railroad accidents were filed separately and there weren't too many of them so it wasn't too difficult to run through and pick out those which had happened in the freight yards. In five years—which was as far back as I checked—there'd been twelve fatal accidents there.

And seven of the twelve I could easily eliminate. There'd been witnesses to them or else they were accidents of such a kind that they couldn't possibly have been deliberately engineered. Another one—a hobo who had died as a result of having both his legs cut off by the wheels of a freight car—I eliminated after I'd read it through to the end and had discovered he'd lived for two days and had regained consciousness. If he'd been pushed, he'd have mentioned it.

But there were four others, all within two years. And any or all—or none—of them could have been what I was looking for.

A hobo had fallen between the cars of a moving train just heading out of the yards and gathering speed. Another had died the same way except that the fall had been between two of a string of cars that were being shunted from one side track to another. In both cases the bodies had been found an hour or two later, badly mangled, but it was possible to reconstruct what had happened by checking car movements and blood on car wheels.

A brakeman, or what was left of him, had been found on the tracks after an entire string of freight cars and the engine pushing it had passed over him. He'd just gone off duty and was on his way back to the office to punch out. Presumably he'd tried to cut across the tracks in front of them and had been run down. But they hadn't been going fast; he must have stumbled and fallen in front of them. Or he could have been pushed or knocked down in front of them.

The fourth accident was to a hobo again. This time there was a witness, in a way, the engineer of the engine that had run over him. He'd been looking out his window and just as the front of the engine, which was going forward and not pushing or pulling any cars, had come level with the end of a string of stationary empties the hobo had run or jumped from behind them right in front of the engine; almost as though he'd done it deliberately, the engineer had said.

Or as though someone standing behind him at the end of the string of stationary cars had given him a sudden push?

All four of those accidents had happened after dark, one as early as eight o'clock in the evening, one as late as two in the morning.

Any one of them could have been an accident. All four of them could have been accidents. So could all of the deaths at the high school, the death at the amusement park. So, I felt sure now, could other deaths in other places.

Where else had Obie hunted?

· 3 ·

I went back downstairs to the non-traffic accident files.

Working backwards chronologically I started going through them. A quick glance at each was enough for most of them. If there were no witnesses I looked to see

how the accident happened and if there were witnesses
I looked for one name among them. Not expecting to
find that name, really, but on the off chance that once
Obie might have made a kill and not been able to get
away fast enough to keep from being corralled as a witness, probably the only witness. I was looking for a case
in which, say, a man had fallen to his death from the
roof of a building and maybe other witnesses had seen
him land but only one had seen him fall—a boy who'd
been on the roof with him, a boy named Henry or Obie
Westphal, who'd seen the victim walk to the edge to
look down and then lose his balance.

By noon I'd looked at hundreds of files and had gone
back almost three years and hadn't found anything. After
a while I'd quit looking to see how accidents had happened unless there were names of witnesses to them.
There were too many that had happened to people who
were alone or presumed to be alone and which could
have resulted from a sudden strategic push if someone
had been there to give it and then run. I wasn't going to
let myself get psychopathic about this thing—unless I
already was—and start suspecting Obie in every apparently accidental death that could conceivably have been
a kill instead. He couldn't have killed *all* of them.

Chief Steiner's secretary wasn't at his desk when I
went out to eat lunch but he was there when I came back.

"Finding any good cases for your article?" he asked
me.

"A few," I said. "But it's tough going; most accidents
are pretty routine. I'll have to dig back more years than
I thought to find enough screwy ones."

"Uh-huh. Say, an uncle of mine died in a screwy type
of accident once. Maybe you can use it. Fell and killed
himself because of termites in his wooden leg."

"You're kidding me."

"I'm not. He'd used a wooden leg for several years
after an amputation, then got a new aluminum one, put

the old one out in a shed. Couple of years later something
went wrong with the new leg and he went out and got
the old one to use till he could get the new one fixed.
Put it on and it broke under him half an hour later and
pitched him down a flight of stairs. Termites had eaten
most of the inside of it away.''

"That I'll *have* to use.''

"Better look it up and be sure I'm right on the details.
You'll find it in the drawer for—let's see, it was around
twelve or thirteen years ago. Nineteen forty-one or nineteen forty. His name was Andrew Wilson; look it up in
the yearly alphabetical list for one of those two years,
the list at the front of the drawer.''

"I'll do that. Thanks a lot.''

I went back to the files and spent a couple of hours
going back another couple of years. No luck.

It had been a wasted day thus far except for what I'd
found in the traffic accident files upstairs, those four
accidents within two years at the freight yards. All of
them, in the light of what I knew and suspected, looking
pretty fishy to me. Of course I'd probably not have given
them a second thought if it hadn't been that Obie had
gone there the evening I'd followed him.

Still, nothing to get my teeth into. No proof of Obie's
connection with any supposedly accidental death except
that of Jimmy Chojnacki, and there the only direct proof
was the presence of Obie's wallet in Jimmy's pocket
when he died. And the lunch counter man's story that
placed Obie at his stand just before the accident and gone
at the time the accident happened.

I'd hate to try to convince anyone else on evidence
like that.

I started away from the files and then turned back. I'd
better carry out my pretext by looking up the report on
the death of the secretary's uncle; he might ask me something about it when I passed his desk on the way out.

I pulled open the 1939 drawer and took out the al-

phabetical list. Half a dozen W's on it, but no Wilson.
But it was in the alphabetical list in the 1940 drawer;
Andrew Wilson, and the date. I looked up the report and
read it; the secretary hadn't been kidding me. Termites
in a wooden leg. Maybe, I thought, I really should write
that article on screwy accidents. Andrew Wilson would
make a damned good lead for it.

I started out again, got almost to the door, and stopped
as though I'd walked into something solid. Hadn't one
of those names under W in the first drawer I'd looked
in, the 1939 drawer, been *Westphal?*

Well, what if it had, I asked myself. My God, in 1939
Obie would have been four years old. And besides, those
alphabetical lists for each year were lists of the names
of *victims* of fatal accidents, not witnesses or others involved. It must be just a coincidence. Westphal is not
too uncommon a name.

I went back to the drawer and looked at the list again.
Westphal, Elizabeth, April 16.

I fumbled a little finding the file; I went past it in the
chronological sequence and had to go back. Then I had
it in my hand, a thin manila file folder with only three
sheets of paper in it. I flipped it open and glanced at the
top sheet, a copy of the death certificate signed by Dr.
Lawrence J. Wygand. I knew him.

*Elizabeth Westphal, age 5 yrs., daughter of Mr. and
Mrs. Armin Westphal, 314 S. Rampart St. . . . .*

I closed the folder and the file drawer; I took the folder
over to the window and sat down on the sill. I stared at
the folder, almost afraid to open it.

This, I thought, might be the key I was looking
for. But could it? In 1939 Obie would have been four
years old.

But he hadn't been an only child. Grace Smith had
been wrong about that. He'd had a sister a year older
than himself.

She had died—accidentally.

I took a deep breath and opened the folder.

The death certificate was a photostat of the original. Cause of death; severing of spinal cord between the first and second lumbar vertebrae. Other indications; severe contusions and lacerations of back, left forearm and right calf. Time of death: approximately 3:10 P.M. Time of physician's examination: 3:15 P.M.

The next two pages consisted of a typed report of a routine investigation of the accident, signed by a Lieutenant John Carpenter.

The five-year-old girl and her four-year-old brother— called Henry in the report—had been playing in the back yard of the Westphal house on Rampart Street and had both climbed into a tree near the back fence. They had never been told not to climb it for it was a tree they could not ordinarily have got into; its lowest branches were well out of reach and the trunk too big around for them to climb. But Mr. Westphal had been pruning the tree and had left a stepladder leaning against the trunk. By means of the stepladder it had been easy for the children to climb into the tree and both Mr. and Mrs. Westphal were inside the house and were unaware that the children had done so.

Mr. Westphal had been upstairs and had happened to look out a back window to see what the children were doing and had seen them in the tree. Just as he was about to throw open the window to call to them to be careful and stay where they were until he could come to help them safely down, Elizabeth fell out of the tree. She landed on her back across the fence and from there on into the alley behind the yard. She had screamed while she was falling.

Mr. Westphal had rushed down the stairs. Mrs. Westphal was in the living room, running the vacuum cleaner; the sound of it had kept her from hearing the scream

from the back yard. Mr. Westphal had yelled at her to
phone Dr. Wygand to rush around fast. He had run on
out into the alley and found Elizabeth unconscious, probably already dead. He had carried her into the house and
put her on a sofa. He and Mrs. Westphal were still trying
to find a heartbeat or a sign of life when the doctor arrived
and pronounced her dead. Neither of the Westphals had
looked at a clock nor had Dr. Wygand when he received
the emergency call but the time of the accident was
established within a minute or so because the doctor had
looked at his watch when he made the death pronounce-
ment. It was then 3:15 P.M. Dr. Wygand also lived on
Rampart Street, less than a block away, and it had taken
him only two or three minutes to get there; allowing a
minute for the phone call and another minute or two after
his arrival before he had glanced at his watch, the accident had happened about five minutes before. The doctor had stated that, in all probability, death had been
instantaneous.

The fence across which the girl had fallen was a board
fence five feet high; the limb of the tree from which she
had fallen was about twenty feet from the ground, about
fifteen feet from the top of the fence.

The boy, Henry, had said that his sister had climbed
the tree first and he had followed her. He had been
astraddle of the limb just behind her; she had tried to
hold onto the limb with her legs only and had reached
both hands above her head to try to catch the limb above
but had lost her balance in doing so. He had tried to grab
at her and had managed to touch her but not to hold on.

He had got down from the tree safely and under his
own power while Mr. Westphal had been coming down
the stairs and running to Elizabeth in the alley.

Mr. Westphal had been unable to verify his son's story
of exact details of how the girl had fallen. He had seen
the children through a partial screen of branches and

leaves so he had not had a clear view of what had happened. But the boy had seemed quite intelligent for his age and there was no reason to doubt his version of how his sister had happened to fall, the lieutenant who wrote the report stated. He added, gratuitously, that it was probably well the boy had not succeeded in grabbing his sister; otherwise they would both have fallen.

That was all.

I put back the folder and closed the file drawer.

I left, and luckily the secretary wasn't at his desk when I passed it, so I didn't have to stop and talk about termites to him.

There's a bar almost directly across the street from police headquarters and I headed there and ordered myself a beer. I wanted a chance to think.

I had something, but I didn't know what I had. Can a four-year-old boy commit murder?

Or could it be that Obie hadn't pushed his sister but their father had *thought* he had? Suddenly a new possibility occurred to me: What if Armin Westphal, and not Obie, was psychotic? What if Obie had never killed anyone but Armin Westphal had the delusion that his son was a killer, a delusion that dated from the death of his daughter? Wouldn't that account for his paying for the funeral of Johnny Chojnacki? If Westphal was psychotic—

·4·

Suddenly I wanted to know all I could learn about Armin Westphal. Maybe Doc Wygand could tell me something. I went to the phone booth at the back of the tavern and phoned him.

"Sam Evans, Doc," I said. "Going to be home about half an hour from now and free to talk awhile?"

He chuckled. "Free and getting bored. Come on out, Sam. Don't know if you knew, but I retired three months ago. Almost beginning to wish I hadn't."

"Be right out," I said.

I finished my beer on my way past the bar, then I went out and got in the Buick and drove to Rampart Street. The telephone directory had told me he still lived in the same place. He'd been a close friend of my parents and I'd liked him a lot too, although I hadn't seen him often since their deaths.

He was dressed in disreputable old clothes and working in his garden when I got there. He took off canvas gloves to shake hands and said it was good to see me again. "Nothing wrong, is there, Sam? I mean, I hope you didn't want to see me professionally, did you? If so, we'll just forget that I retired and—"

"No, Doc, I'm feeling fine. Just want to ask some questions about a case you had once."

He sighed. "Almost hoping you had something wrong with you. Shall we go inside to talk or would you rather go over there?" He gestured toward some garden furniture in the shade of a big oak tree. I chose the shade of the tree and we went over and made ourselves comfortable.

"Still working for the *Herald*, Sam?"

"Yes, but I'm on vacation this week. So what I want to ask you about is something I'm interested in personally. It—well, it could lead to a newspaper story if it breaks, but I'll promise not to quote you or use your name if that happens."

"Ummm, but don't forget that a physician can't reveal— Well, go ahead and ask your questions. I'll have to decide whether I can answer them or not. What's the case?"

"A girl named Elizabeth Westphal who fell out of a tree, right in this block, a neighbor of yours."

"Yes, I remember. Armin Westphal's kid, must have been at least ten years ago. What do you want to know about her?"

"Not the medical details. Everything but that. Family background in particular, what you know about other members of the family, in particular."

"Good, then I won't have to watch what I say at all. I knew the Westphals when they lived here—haven't seen Armin very often since—but none of them were ever patients of mine. Except that time when the little girl was killed, and she was dead when I got there so there's no medical confidence involved there; I can even talk about that."

"All right," I said, "let's start with that, then. One question in particular. Did you get the impression that Armin Westphal may have thought his son deliberately pushed his sister out of that tree?"

Doc had been leaning back comfortably. He sat up straight now and stared at me. But he thought for seconds before he answered.

"No," he said. "Good God, why would he have thought that?"

"He saw it happen. Not too good a view because there were leaves and branches in the way, so he might have thought he saw Obie—Henry—push his sister off the limb and yet not have been sure enough of what he saw to say so—even if he *would* have said so about his own son."

Doc leaned back again in his chair. "It's just barely possible, Sam, now that I think back. Armin did react to his daughter's death in a way that was a little different from and in addition to normal grief. But I interpreted it otherwise—and I still think I was right. I thought he blamed himself and was building a guilt complex."

"Why would he have blamed himself?"

"Two reasons. The first one, minor, his carelessness in leaving that ladder against the tree. If he hadn't left it there the kids wouldn't have been climbing in the tree; they couldn't have. That's silly, of course. But the other reason isn't. There's a chance, a pretty damn small one, that he *did* kill his daughter by picking her up and carrying her into the house. You don't do that to someone with a broken back."

"How small a chance, mathematically?"

"I thought it was a pretty fair chance at first. I'm afraid I almost lost my temper with him for his stupidity in moving her before I got there. But then I went out into the yard and looked over the scene of the accident and learned how it happened and I realized that it was almost impossible for her to have been alive when he reached her."

"Why?"

"Because she'd fallen on her back on top of the fence and then had another fall of five feet to the ground. The top of the fence had broken her back; the nature of the injury showed that clearly. A broken back, though, isn't necessarily a fatal injury; lots of people live with broken backs. But when the broken vertebra or vertebrae cut or too seriously injure the spinal cord that runs through the vertebrae, death is pretty damn quick. Now Elizabeth's back was so badly broken—imagine falling fifteen feet and taking all of the impact diagonally across your back on the narrow top of a fence—that the chances are a thousand to one she was killed there and then. But with a back that badly broken she'd sustained an additional five-foot fall into a concrete alley. If the top of the fence hadn't killed her there was another one chance in a thousand that the impact of the second fall, with her back already badly broken, wouldn't have killed her. There's your mathematical answer, incidentally; figure the permutation of two thousand-to-one chances and you get a one-in-a-million chance.''

"Did you tell Westphal that?"

"By that time my temper was gone and I went even a little farther than that to reassure him. Why give a man who's already on the road to being neurotic something to build a guilt complex around, on a million-to-one chance that he had been guilty? I told him there was no doubt whatsoever—which, for practical purposes there wasn't—that Elizabeth had been dead by the time he moved her.''

"You say he was on the road to being a neurotic. Just what do you mean, Doc?"

His shaggy white eyebrows lifted. "Didn't you know he's an alcoholic? I thought you knew *something* about him.''

"Not much. I didn't know what you just told me. Listen, why not start from scratch, from whenever you knew him first, and give me the works?''

"All right, but I'm dry. Wait till I get us some cold lemonade; there's some ready in the refrigerator. Or would you rather have beer? There's some beer cold too.''

I told him I'd just had a beer and would rather stick to that.

He got us each a can of beer and made himself comfortable again. He said, "Let's see, I've lived here twenty years. Armin built the house at three-fourteen about five years after I bought this one. I got to know him slightly while he was building it.''

"Did he own his store then?"

"No, he was a traveling salesman for a hosiery company. Did very well at it, made good money. You wouldn't think to look at him that he'd be a good salesman but he must be—or at least must have been. He was already, in addition to building his own house, planning on going in business for himself.

"I didn't get to know his family until they moved in after the house was ready. Amy—that's his wife—and the two children, Elizabeth and Henry, one year apart. Let's see, they'd have been three and two years old then, or about that. I noticed you called the boy Obie a few minutes ago; he didn't get that nickname until around the time he started high school. You know it comes from his middle name, Obadiah?"

I nodded.

"Well, my wife and I got to know them fairly well after they moved in. They weren't really close friends but we played bridge with them once in a while. Never had 'em as patients, though. They already had a family doctor and besides I believe Armin thought I was a little fusty and old-fashioned.

"Armin was quite a heavy drinker even then. Maybe not quite an alcoholic yet, but close to it. That means there was some hidden conflict in him somewhere, but I didn't get to know him well enough even to make a guess what it was. But it was later, after Elizabeth's death, that his drinking definitely took on the pattern of alcoholism. There are different types of alcoholics, you know; Armin's the periodic type. Doesn't touch the stuff for months at a time, sometimes as long as eight or nine months, although six would be nearer average, and then he's off on a drinking bout and won't come home for a week or two, once that I know of as long as three weeks. Refuses to be cured, won't go to a san unless it's just for a brief rest cure to get his health back after an unusually bad bout."

"You're sure he's still that way?"

"Yes. His last one was only four or five months ago. I haven't seen him that recently, but I happened to hear about it from a mutual acquaintance."

"What do you know about Mrs. Westphal?"

"Amy's a fine woman. Not overweight mentally but,

as far as shows on the outside, a good wife and mother. Well, maybe too good a mother, the kind that dotes too much on children and spoils them. And Henry got a double dose of it after he became an only child, but I guess he came through okay. I've heard he's quite a football hero in high school. Well, if his mother's spoiling him didn't turn his head, that probably won't either.''

"When did you see him last?''

"Quite a few years ago. He was in the fourth or fifth grade of elementary school then. Matter of fact, I saw him only a few times after they moved away from Rampart Street.''

"And when was that? And, if you know, why?''

"It would have been in—ummm—nineteen forty-three. As to why, I'd say it was a combination of reasons. It wasn't just because their daughter had been killed there—they wouldn't have stayed four more years if that was the only reason—but they didn't like the place so well after that. And in nineteen forty-three there was the war boom and the housing shortage; Armin was able to sell for just about double what the place had cost him to build six years before, during the depression. He used that profit to set himself up in business, to start his store downtown. And I understand he's done well with it.''

"Tell me one thing, Doc. After Elizabeth's death, did you notice any change in Westphal's attitude toward the boy?''

He looked at me sharply. "Are we back to the idea that Armin may have thought Henry pushed his sister out of the tree deliberately?''

"Let's say I'm still trying it for size.''

"All right, I guess the best answer I can give you is that I probably wouldn't have noticed any difference, unless it showed damned plainly. For one thing, I wasn't looking for it. For another I didn't see much of the two together. If we played cards with the Westphals, it was generally at our place because, being in active practice, I wanted to be available for phone calls. And they had a maid who lived there, so there wasn't any worry about baby sitters on their end.

"But come to think of it, I don't remember Armin talking much about Henry after that, if at all. And he probably *was* different with the boy because he was different with everyone. That's when he started to get moody and—well, definitely neurotic."

"Did he ever play with the boy, take him places?"

"Why—not that I remember specifically, after that accident."

"But he did before that?"

"Yes, he'd take Henry for walks, play with him in the yard, things like that. You know, Sam, maybe you've got something at that. The more I think of it the more I think maybe his attitude toward Henry did change then. I mean, even more than he started changing in general. Mind telling me what this is all about? Not that I insist on it if you'd rather not."

"I'd really rather not, Doc, if you'll forgive me. Someday maybe, but not right now."

"Sure. How's Millie these days?"

"Fine," I said, and let it go at that. I didn't want to talk about Millie. So I asked him some questions that got him talking about his garden. It was five o'clock when, with the story that I had to go home to dress for a dinner engagement, I managed to get away and to forestall being pressed to stay and eat with him.

A fine guy, Doc; my parents had shown good judgment in choosing their friends. I wonder, now that it's all over, if I'll ever tell him the truth. I don't think so. It can't do any good, and there's no reason to.

·5·

Because I wanted to be alone to think things out again, I went home. I couldn't have picked a lonesomer place for it. And I'd been stupid to come home before eating because there wasn't anything to eat here and I'd have to go out soon again anyway. I wasn't hungry yet but I'd get that way sooner or later and I didn't want to interrupt myself once I started, so I walked the two blocks to the neighborhood delicatessen and bought rolls and sandwich meat and some pickles. Nothing to drink. I was going to figure things out cold sober.

Back home I found the walk had given me enough appetite to make and eat a couple of sandwiches so I got that over with. Then I got an old card table from the basement and set it up in front of the most comfortable chair in the living room to put my feet on. I think best with my feet up.

I sat down and put my feet up.

There were two main possibilities and I had to think each of them through and decide which one was probably right.

One, maybe Obie *wasn't* a killer. I'd been sure he was until this afternoon, but what I'd just learned opened up a completely new line of thought.

Armin Westphal was at least neurotic, any alcoholic is. But maybe he was farther off the beam than that. Starting with the death of his five-year-old daughter, he could have built up a systematized delusion that his son was a murderer—without any basis in reality except something he *thought* he saw thirteen years ago.

Or he could even have seen Obie push his sister with-

out having witnessed a deliberate killing. Murder by a
four-year-old would be something damned unusual, but
lying by a four-year-old isn't; Obie's story of how his
sister happened to fall might quite easily have been pure
invention to avoid punishment. He'd said, for instance,
that she'd climbed the tree first. A natural thing for him
to say when it turned out that climbing the tree had been
wrong. And the rest of the story could have been a
protective lie too. Maybe they'd been scuffling in fun.
Or even *not* in fun; suppose Obie had climbed the tree
alone first and then, as a joke, dropped something on
his sister's head. She'd climbed up quickly to slap him
and—

Yes, there were dozens of ways in which the scene in
the tree could have so happened that Westphal could
have thought he saw Obie push his sister out. Or he could
have genuinely seen Obie push her accidentally. And he
could have known that Obie's story of what had happened
up there was a lie and assumed it to be a deadly lie
instead of a protective fib.

Now add that to his own guilt feelings for having left
the ladder by the tree and for having been so stupid in
his excitement that he'd picked up Elizabeth and carried
her when, after seeing how she'd landed on the fence,
a broken back was a virtual certainty. Suppose that,
despite the doctor's reassurance after his initial bawling
out, Westphal still felt responsible for his daughter's
death. The human mind, even one that isn't neurotic,
can take devious ways to duck or shift responsibility.
Such as, in Westphal's case, shifting the blame to his
son, becoming more and more convinced that his son
was a murderer.

Watching him from that moment on, suspicion growing into certainty and certainty growing into obsession.
Seeing confirmation of his obsession in a thousand words
and actions completely normal to childhood. *The toy*

pistol. "*Bang, bang, you're dead.*" The cowboy stage. Cops and robbers.

Children *are* killers—in their fantasies. Killing is as natural to them as breathing, and as free of malice. Swords and six-guns and Buck Rogers blasters and the staccato chatter of the machine gun. What boy, from five to ten, doesn't kill thousands, sometimes thousands in a single day, in his mental world where every bullet hits and every shot is fatal? With every *bang* another redskin bites the dust, another cop, another robber, another enemy soldier, another Martian. The collective killings in our nurseries could depopulate the world in a single day, the universe within a week. It's the catharsis that lets childhood rid itself of the bloodlust that is our heritage from mankind's past when bloodlust was necessary to survival.

But God help an obsessed man who'd watch his son playing for confirmation of his obsession that the boy was a psychopathic killer who had killed once and might kill again.

Bang, bang, bang.

And real death? Well, it doesn't take much to feed an obsession. Any accidental death that happened for miles around and which, even remotely, barely possibly *could* have been caused by a boy of whatever age Obie was at the time would have been looked on by Westphal with dark suspicion. Where there was reasonable possibility— like the accidents at high school—that Obie could have been guilty, Westphal's obsession would make him certain.

As he'd been certain that Obie had killed Jimmy Chojnacki and without knowing, or at least before learning, any of the details of the accident except that there'd been an erroneous preliminary identification because Obie's wallet had been in the pocket of the dead boy.

Well, I'd come to believe the same thing myself, hadn't

I? But not until I'd learned at least *some* of the details,
and not until I'd watched Westphal's face as he'd entered
the funeral parlor thinking his son was dead, watched it
again when he'd left knowing that his son was alive and
waiting for him at home, even then not until I'd gone in
and talked to Haley, my curiosity aroused by Westphal's
unnatural behavior, and had learned that Westphal had
volunteered to pay for a pickpocket's funeral.

My main reason for suspecting Obie had been his
father's reactions. And what I'd learned today had given
me a possible, maybe a probable explanation that left
Obie innocent; I'd been led astray by the delusions of a
paranoiac.

Yes, but what about the story of the lunch-stand man
that placed Obie so near the place at so near the time of
the death?

I'd already thought of—and discarded as improbable—another explanation of how Jimmy could have died.
It seemed less improbable now. *Obie missing his wallet,
turning and seeing Jimmy heading back over the fence
giving chase. Jimmy trying to beat the cars across the
track because he was trying to escape.*

And with what I knew now I could make a guess as
to the rest of it, Obie's reason for making himself scarce
before the body was found, for not waiting and telling
how it had really happened. Obie must know of his
father's suspicions of him. He'd have known that his
father, if no one else, would never believe his story,
without proof except his own word, that Jimmy's death
had been accidental. He'd have run away without thinking twice. Later, of course, he'd have remembered that
Jimmy had still had his wallet; he'd realize that to avoid
suspicion it would be necessary for him to go to the Lost
and Found Department and ask for it. But he'd waited
a few hours, for things to cool down, before he'd gone
there. Never guessing, of course, that since Jimmy had

carried no identification of his own a mistake in identification would cause his, Obie's, parents to be notified
that their son was dead.

That explanation made sense now.

And what did I have besides that? The coincidence of
four deaths within three years at the high school? But
I'd already learned that one of those four, the drowning
of a girl in a girls' swimming period, couldn't possibly
have been caused by Obie. And that the other drowning,
the teacher Constance Bonner, seemed quite probably a
suicide and anyway didn't really fit the pattern of the
type of killing I'd pictured Obie doing.

Four accidents within two years in the freight yards?
All four of them could have fitted the pattern, yes, but
why should I think Obie caused them just because he'd
gone there the one evening I'd followed him. There'd
been no accident there that particular night. And there
were at least a dozen reasons, legitimate ones, for his
having walked there. A randomly chosen objective for
a pleasant stroll on a warm summer night. A destination,
such as a friend's house, beyond the yards, and a short
cut through them. A human and unmurderous interest in
hoboes. An adventurous interest in railroads and a pre-
dilection for hopping and riding moving freight cars.

So what did I have left? Nothing that couldn't be
explained away by mild coincidence.

And yet—

I wasn't sitting with my feet up any more now. I'd
got my start thinking that way, but now I was pacing.
I'd pushed the card table aside and I had the whole length
of the living room to pace in. It's a good room for pacing,
narrow but longish.

And yet, I thought, *I've got a much better case against
Obie than I had before. If he is a killer, I can see why.*

The other side of the coin my friend the doctor had
handed me.

In what dark way might a boy react to his father's belief that he was a murderer?

Let's start it that way from the crisis point, the death of Elizabeth Westphal. No, I still wouldn't follow Westphal there, no matter what he might have seen in the tree. A four-year-old boy as a deliberate murderer, that I wouldn't buy. But I could see a boy warped into becoming one, over the course of the years of his formative period, by his father's unwavering belief.

Let's say he had pushed his sister. In play, in a scuffle, maybe in defense because she was trying to push him. In whatever manner, for whatever reason, but not to kill her. In his story of what had happened, he lied a little bit, naturally. He daren't admit that he had pushed her; he was trying to save her, but couldn't.

But then he learns that his father had *seen* that push. His father thinks he is a murderer. His father keeps on thinking so, more and more strongly as the years go by. The years, let us say, from four to thirteen. Nine years of being thought a murderer, nine years of being *watched*, of feeling and being made to feel that he is unnatural, a freak, a thing to be feared and hated.

And likely, for that very reason, he *didn't* indulge in the normal killings-in-fantasy of childhood. Certainly not at any time when his father was around watching him. His father's brooding, watching, somber gaze—under that, would he ever dare point a finger and say *bang*, even at the most imaginary Indian, let alone at a living playmate? Would his father ever have bought him a toy gun, a cap pistol, a rubber knife, *any* of the pseudo-lethal things normal to boyhood?

If he ever said or even thought "Bang, bang, you're dead" it would have been in secret and with a feeling of deep guilt because death and killing were real to him; he had already killed, in reality, and thereby he was denied the catharsis of the imaginary mowing down of enemies.

He had killed his sister. Oh yes, he would have come, by the age of eleven or twelve or thirteen, to believe that. How accurately does anyone remember the details of and the motives behind any act he committed at the age of four, years later?

A month or two after the incident, he would still have remembered that the push had been in fun, in play. Even then, he wouldn't have been sure. And eight or nine years later? By then the true memory would have been supplanted by a false one, so firmly imbedded that any other version would have been sheer fantasy.

And how he must have come to fear and hate his father! But probably the fear and hate would be buried deep, buried under layers of guilt and awful knowledge of his own viciousness and abnormality.

Henry the murderer, Henry the unspeakable.

Obie the hero, Obie the athlete, the lionized, the admired.

Henry the murderer, Obie the hero.

Schizophrenia.

All right, all right, I told myself, I'm guessing of course. I haven't got enough, I don't know enough to do these parlor tricks with psychoanalysis. I'm guessing.

Well, what's wrong with guessing, as long as I don't wear a groove in the carpet while I'm doing it?

Of course there'd been a balance to Armin Westphal. What had Doc told me about Obie's mother?

Amy's a fine woman. Not overweight mentally . . . a good wife and mother. Well, maybe too good a mother, the kind that dotes too much on children and spoils them. And Henry got a double dose of it after he became an only child. . . .

Certainly not overweight mentally if she failed to recognize the symptoms of her husband's mental illness, to feel the weight of his obsession, however devious he was in concealing it from her.

She must, of course, have felt at least inadequacy in

his attitude toward his son, but there was so simple and natural an answer to that. Love the boy twice as much herself, spoil him, be wonderful to him in every possible way to make up to him the apparent lack of love his father showed for him. Of course, Armin didn't *really* feel that way, and although sometimes Henry seemed almost—well, almost *afraid* of his father and was so quiet when his father was around, that was just his way. And although Armin's way of showing it was strange, he must love his son deep down and deeply else why would he *watch* the boy so much and so intently. Why would he ask him so many questions? Mostly when she wasn't around, but that was natural; men didn't want women around when they did their serious talking. She had a wonderful son—so big and handsome for his age, so smart in school, so admired by everyone. And she had a wonderful husband, if only he could get over that awful drinking, and if only he didn't act so strangely sometimes. But then he worked so hard, for all of them.

She must have spoiled the boy terribly after he became her only child. And like as not Oedipus had reared his head somewhere in those years, although God knows Obie wouldn't have needed jealousy of his mother to make him hate his father, if I had the picture right.

Meanwhile growing up, gaining wisdom and stature. From the size of him now, he might have been as strong as a man at thirteen. Able, maybe, to lick his own father—and certainly able to now at seventeen—but afraid to. That's the one thing he'd always be afraid to do.

I'd guess thirteen to be the age at which Obie made his first kill. In his own mind, convinced by then that he had killed his sister, believing that for nine years, it would have been his second. Why did I pick thirteen? I don't know; it could have been sooner than that, much sooner. Not more than a year later, though, if the two boys who had died at South Side during his freshman year had been his victims.

The first kill, especially, must have been unplanned. Maybe all of them were—although his visit to the freight yards looked as though he hunted opportunities.

He'd have been in some dangerous place, say on a roof, with one other person. No one else around, no one watching. The other person—friend or stranger, it wouldn't matter—standing near the edge, Obie behind him. And it would come to him: *Why, just a push and I could kill him easily, just as I killed my sister.*

Suddenly the blood had pounded in his temples, and he had pushed. He had killed.

Whom had he killed? His father, of course. The one being he wanted to kill and feared to kill, he killed in effigy. And killed in effigy again and again, any time a foolproof opportunity came or could be contrived.

Did he know that, I wondered; did he know whom he killed? Or did his subconscious mind hide that dark fact from his conscious one? Did he know only the sudden savage delight each killing gave him, without recognizing the source of that wild ecstasy?

All right, Sam, I told myself, you've got two perfectly good solutions and which one do you like best?

One, Obie's killings are the delusion of a paranoiac father.

Two, Obie's killings are the result of his father's obsession.

Pay your money and take your choice.

Either fitted.

And I wanted to kick furniture through the windows because I didn't know which. I wanted to kick myself because I couldn't simply accept the first one, which was just as possible as the second. Because if I could accept that I'd merely been fooled by Westphal into momentary sharing of his delusion, then I was through with this thing and it would be off my mind.

I wouldn't have to do a damned thing about it except forget it. It would mean Westphal was insane, but that wasn't any business of mine. Not if it hadn't made a killer out of his son. Not if all those deaths at the school and in the jungles had really been accidents, and if Jimmy Chojnacki had really fallen across the tracks because he'd been running away from a pursuer.

But how the hell could I decide? The only one of those deaths that was fresh was that of the Chojnacki boy and I'd dug into that as hard and as far as I knew how to dig. All of the others were months or years ago and how could I possibly connect Obie with any of them now?

Wait, I told myself, you've been wondering how to prove that Obie caused those deaths, or some of them, and maybe that's impossible, but why not try it from the other end? Maybe I could prove that Obie hadn't caused them.

It would be difficult if not impossible, now, to find proof that Obie had been elsewhere at the times of the freight-yard accidents. But I might be able to prove that he couldn't have caused any of the three accidents still under suspicion at the school.

There was an even chance, for instance, that I could prove he hadn't pushed the Greenough boy out of the tower window. Nina had told me it had happened during second lunch period. The school day at South Side is divided into eight three-quarter-hour periods. Schedules are so arranged that approximately half of the students have their lunch time during the fifth period, from 12:00 noon to 12:45 P.M. and the other half during the sixth period, from 12:45 to 1:30 P.M. Otherwise the school cafeteria couldn't handle them. But suppose Obie's schedule for his freshman year gave him first lunch period and a class at the time the Greenough boy had fallen?

And if, that same year, Obie had not had a final period gym class, it would become highly unlikely that he had killed the Negro boy in the locker room. Not impossible; he could have gone to the locker room in the gym after some other last-period class so it wouldn't give him a complete alibi, but it would lessen probability. Or he might have been absent from school completely on one of those days. Attendance records would show.

As for the teacher Constance Bonner, well, that was probably a suicide anyway. But I could almost completely rule out Obie if I could learn from his record that he didn't belong to the Drama Club during his junior year. Only the members of that group, whom she had let out of the building when the meeting was over, would have known that Miss Bonner had stayed there to grade papers.

Nina could find those things out for me from the school records. I hated to ask her to because I couldn't without telling her at least part of the truth about what I was after and without admitting that I'd been lying about my reason for asking the questions I'd already asked her about the accidents. She'd place those dates and times and know that I was trying to connect Obie Westphal with those three deaths. And she'd remember that I'd already asked her casually whether Obie and Jimmy Chojnacki had been friends.

But I didn't see any way I could find out those things except through Nina.

I looked at my watch and it was nine o'clock. She'd said she was going to bed early to get a long night's sleep, but surely she'd hardly have turned in this early.

I phoned her. It even came to me, as I heard the number ringing, that maybe she'd be feeling differently by now and want me to come around to stay the night. After all, after three nights in a row I wouldn't keep us up *very* late tonight.

"Hello."

"This is Sam, Nina. Still annoyed with me?"

"I wasn't annoyed with you, Sam. It's just—I was being sensible for once."

"Still feeling sensible, darling?"

She laughed a little. "No, I'm not. I was hoping you'd call. I was afraid you were annoyed with *me* for being so silly this morning. I want you to come around, dear. But—"

"Oh, no," I said.

"Oh, yes, I'm afraid. It started today, Sam, two days early. So I'm going to be a good girl and get to bed early whether I want to or not."

"But you don't have to turn in *this* early do you, Nina? There's something I want you to do for me. Well, there *were* two things but now we can rule out one of them. Can I, though, drop over for just a little while? A half hour, maybe? I'm calling from home and I can be there in twenty minutes."

"Please don't, Sam. I'm really dead tired; I'd just turned in when the phone rang. Another three minutes and I'd have been too sound asleep to have heard it. Whatever it is you want me to do, I'm afraid I couldn't. I'm half asleep now."

"It's nothing for you to do tonight. I just wanted to explain it to you so you could do it tomorrow."

"Can't you tell me over the phone?"

"It's—I'm afraid it's too complicated for that."

"Then can't it wait a day, Sam? Please?"

"All right," I said. "Go to bed and pound your pretty ear. Good night."

"Good night, darling."

"Will I see you tomorrow night?"

"If you wish, after what I just told you."

"Don't be a goof," I said. "If you think my wanting to see you is for one reason only, I'm glad of a chance to prove otherwise. And how's about my taking you out to dinner for a change? Will you be ready at—say, half past six?"

"But—aren't you worried about someone seeing us together?"

"Of course not. But if you are—and I suppose that, working for the school board, it wouldn't do you any good to be seen with a married man—we can drive out to some place in the country where there wouldn't be a chance in a thousand of either of us seeing someone who knows him."

"I think it's better that way. Yes, I'd love to, Sam. I'll be ready at six-thirty. And thanks for skipping tonight; I'll be sound asleep in minutes. 'Night, darling."

"Good night, Nina."

"Love me—just a little bit?"

"What other possible motive could I have for feeding you tomorrow evening?"

She laughed, and we said good night again and hung up.

I wasn't sleepy and I decided I wanted a drink before I turned in, maybe several drinks. I wanted to quit thinking, too. I'd have to wait a day now to have Nina get me the dope from the school files that might help me make up my mind about Obie, and maybe it would be a good thing for me to forget it for a day. Damn it, this was my vacation.

And besides, I wanted to talk to someone. About anything except the family Westphal.

I drove to the Press Bar across the street from the *Herald*. It was Thursday night now; I wouldn't have any trouble explaining to the boys why I was in town. I could simply say that five days on the lake had been enough and that I'd come back a little early.

Ordinarily there'd have been anywhere from two to ten people I knew in the Press Bar at nine-thirty on a week night. Tonight, because I wanted company, there wasn't one. Even the bartender must have been a new one; he was a stranger to me.

I drank a few beers, though, and got into a conversation with the man next to me at the bar, but it was a one-sided conversation because he wanted to talk baseball and I know nothing about baseball and care less. But beer and baseball combined to make me sleepy so when I went home and to bed somewhere around eleven o'clock I went to sleep the moment I put my head on the pillow.

FRIDAY

· 1 ·

In my dream I was standing at the end of a swimming pool. The pool was filled not with water but with ink, black ink. Somehow I knew, although of course I couldn't see through the ink, that I was standing at the deep end, just a foot or so from the edge. And in my dream I couldn't swim, although actually I can. Someone or something was standing behind me. I wanted to turn but couldn't. Then there came a whisper from behind me, "Turn now," and I turned. A few feet away stood a creature with the body of a man or boy—a big, strong, young boy in slacks and a white T shirt—and the head of a wolf. The wolf's head whispered, "Don't laugh; your daughter may be inside." Then the wolf's head changed to the head of a tiger and it said, "Turn again, Dick Whittington," and I turned obediently to face the deep end of the dark pool. There was a push in the middle of my back and I started falling into the pool, and woke suddenly before I got there.

I was wide awake and I lay there thinking about that dream and wondering what it could mean. I don't mean that I think dreams have meaning in the Gypsy Dream Book sense nor yet do I follow the Freudians in believing in sex symbolism back of every dream. The only thing in that dream which, to my mind, could have been a sex symbol was the wolf's head and my mind had picked that up from the radiator ornament on the jalopy Obie's friend had driven. Where, of course, it was a deliberate, if adolescent, sex symbol. And the "Don't laugh; your daughter may be inside," phrase was a natural association with the wolf's head; it had been lettered on the same jalopy.

Most of the other things were easy to place, too, although I didn't see how Dick Whittington got in there unless as a random association with the phrase "Turn again"; there's an English nursery rhyme something like "Turn again, Whittington, thrice Lord Mayor of London."

But the body under the wolf's head had been Obie's and the change to a tiger's head was easily explicable; I'd thought of Obie metaphorically as a tiger more than once. The ink—well, that was obvious enough for a newspaperman. True, printer's ink is not a liquid; it's the consistency of thick paste and wouldn't work very well in a swimming pool, but dreams aren't so literal as to insist on a point like that.

And the pool itself and not being able to swim and the push—my mind had picked those things from the death of Constance Bonner, the teacher who had probably committed suicide. The deep end—well, if Obie *had* killed her by pushing her into the pool he'd certainly have chosen the deep end for the purpose. Or maybe my subconscious was telling me that *I* was going off the deep end in regard to the whole thing. And maybe, I thought, my subconscious was all too damned right if that's what it was trying to tell me in the dream.

Meanwhile my body, now that I was awake, was telling me something else. It was telling me that I'd drunk quite a bit of beer and that I'd better go to the bathroom before I went back to sleep.

I got up and went to the bathroom and came back, and I couldn't sleep. I kept thinking about Nina, for one thing, wishing I was with her tonight—even under the circumstances. And wondering whether I loved her;

whether I'd want to marry her if Millie and I broke up. And whether I wanted Millie and me to break up, or whether basically I was still in love with Millie and the affair with Nina was just an affair, wonderful right now, but nothing important or permanent.

But damn it, I didn't *want* to decide that now; I didn't even want to think about it. I wanted to stall, to see what was going to happen, to let the decision come to me instead of my hunting for it. And I should wait until Millie came back and find out what she had decided. If she wanted to try playing house again, I should, in all fairness, be able to give it a try; it wouldn't be a fair try if I'd already decided that I loved Nina more. And if I decided now that I definitely didn't love Nina, then, in fairness to her, I should break things off now before she got too emotionally involved, if she wasn't already, and was hurt. And I didn't want to break things off.

I thought, damn a society that insists on monogamy.

My thoughts went round in circles. Like the horsefly under the ceiling of the editorial room last Saturday. Less than a week ago. It seemed a lot longer than that. But when I'd watched that horsefly I'd never heard of Obie Westphal or Jimmy Chojnacki, and I hadn't seen Nina for so long that I'd almost forgotten about her. Certainly I had no thought of having an affair with her this week. I'd been looking forward to a week of fishing and hunting and poker playing at Lake Laflamme.

Millie still thought that's where I was. Instead, Millie, I'm here, sleeping alone in the bed in which we've had so much happiness. And thinking of you, but of another woman too. Wishing I was with her tonight. But not that she was here, in this bed we've shared, with me. Funny what strange scruples and sentimentalities people have. As though it matters *where* something happens.

And you, Millie, have you tried an extramarital experiment this week of limbo?

I tried to picture Millie with someone else and then wished I hadn't tried; the very thought hurt. Damn the double standard, damn everything, damn not being able to sleep. *Damn* not being able to sleep.

The luminous dial of the clock beside the bed had told me it was two o'clock when I'd wakened from that dream. It told me now that the time was three-ten. I'd been awake an hour and ten minutes, after only three hours' sleep, and I was getting wider and wider awake every minute.

Was Nina by any chance awake now, wondering, worrying?

Was Millie?

Three-sixteen. Millie had mild insomnia occasionally. She had something in capsules that a doctor had prescribed for it. Dormison. Had she taken the bottle of capsules with her or was it still where it usually stood, on the top shelf of the medicine cabinet? I got up and lighted a cigarette and then headed for the bathroom again. The Dormison wasn't there. Millie had taken the bottle with her.

Maybe, I thought, I should hit myself in the head with a hammer. Or a blackjack, except that I didn't have a blackjack. Warm milk might help but there wasn't any milk. Or more beer, but there wasn't any beer in the house, or anything else to drink. Or anything to— Yes, there *was* something to eat. There was still some sandwich meat and two rolls left downstairs from what I'd bought at the delicatessen. Thank God for small favors.

I went downstairs. Made a sandwich. Ate it. Felt wider awake than ever. Damn Millie for taking all of the sleeping capsules with her; she might have left a few. But then she didn't know I'd be home this week and besides I'd never had insomnia.

Until now. Like the stock gag of the nightclub emcee who says other emcees always have stories to tell about things that happen to them on the way to the club, but nothing has ever happened to him on his way to the club. Pause. Until tonight.

And maybe, just maybe, Nina was awake too right now. Why wasn't I a telepath so I could know? In her bed, with my arms around her, my body to hers, I could maybe go to sleep and she could maybe go to sleep. But she probably *was* asleep. Everybody on my side of the world was asleep except me. On the other side of the world it was day and all the Chinamen were awake but I was the only person awake on my side. And I was alone and lonesome and wide awake.

I went back upstairs because I'd left my cigarettes there. I lighted one and sat on the edge of the bed to smoke it. When I finished it, I'd try once more to go back to sleep. Three-fifty now. I'd been awake almost two hours after three hours' sleep on the night on which I was going to catch up with my sleeping. Well, I still could if I ever got back to sleep again; there wasn't any reason why I couldn't sleep as late as I wanted to.

That was a bright spot. Look for the bright spots.

What bright spots? I'd probably never sleep again. No sleep to knit the raveled sleeve of care, and how damn raveled can a sleeve get?

I finished the cigarette and turned out the light. And lay there wide awake with my mind making like a horse-fly. Circling from Millie to Nina and back and again, and I didn't want to think about them because I might come to a decision and I didn't want to.

But I did want to decide about Obie, and why couldn't I think about him? I guess because I'd thought myself out the evening before. I'd lined up two possibilities, the only two I could see, and I'd carried each of them as far as I could with the data I had. Farther, in fact; I'd been doing a lot of guessing too. If I thought about Obie now I'd just be going over the same territory again, my mind

again making like a horsefly, the same horsefly in a
different room.

No use even trying to decide between those two al-
ternatives on Obie until I had more data. I'd have more
data when Nina had checked—

Suddenly I swore to myself, realizing something I
hadn't realized before. Tomorrow—today rather—was
Friday, the last school day of the week. If Nina didn't
get me that information from the school records tomorrow, she wouldn't be able to get it until Monday, three
days from now and my vacation over.

Three days lost, and the only days I'd have completely
free before going back to work and maybe Millie being
home to boot, for a long time. The three days I had left
in which to put in full time following my hunch. Or my
delusion.

I could get up early—or get up now and stay awake;
I might as well—and have breakfast with Nina, explain
to her then.

But it was such a complicated, touchy thing to explain.
Having to admit to her that I'd been lying to her on other
fronts, too; the reason for my interest in the accidents at
the school, my questions about the Chojnacki family.

At *breakfast*? Look what had happened at breakfast
this morning or yesterday morning, Thursday morning.
I was sleeping, or not sleeping, alone tonight because
of it.

No, I didn't want to explain to Nina over breakfast
why I wanted to know if Obie Westphal's class schedules
gave him alibis for murders. In fact, I didn't want to
have to explain that, and admit the lies I'd told already,
to Nina at all.

Why couldn't I get that information myself? Right
now?

There wasn't a night watchman at the high school
building; Nina's story of how the body of Constance

Bonner had been discovered by a squad-car patrol proved that. And they'd investigated only because there was a light on. I knew where the file cabinets of students' records were—or at least where they'd been when I attended school there—and it wasn't in line with any window. I had a little pencil flashlight that I could use without a chance of it being seen from the outside. True, I'd have to break or jimmy a window to get in but there surely wouldn't be any burglar alarm system. And I knew the layout.

Was I kidding myself? Did I have the guts to commit a burglary, even a relatively safe and easy one? A breaking-and-entering, really, since I wouldn't be stealing anything.

I looked at the clock. Ten minutes after four. An hour and a half, maybe, until dawn. And I could dress in ten minutes, be there in another twenty. For three precious days.

I still didn't know if I was kidding myself. But I got out of bed and dressed, fast. I was in my car, driving, in less than ten minutes and what with the emptiness of the streets at that hour I made the trip in only fifteen minutes, and without speeding.

I drove past, making sure the building was completely dark, and parked a block and a half away. I checked that I had the things I'd picked up on my way out of the house: the pencil flashlight, a handful of rags in case I had to break glass, a small crowbar. The crowbar was going to be a problem to carry. I solved the problem, though. One end was curved so I dropped it down inside my trousers with the curved end hooked over my belt. With my suit coat buttoned, it wouldn't show. But it banged uncomfortably against my right leg just above the knee when I walked.

I walked back to the school without having seen a person or a car. I took a good look around, and a good listen to make sure no car was coming, before I cut back across the grass and got behind the trees and shrubbery on the west side of the building. That would be the best side because the cover was better and because, too, the windows were better situated. The bottom of the lowest row of windows on that side was just flush with the ground and the windows couldn't be seen at all from the street. If I'd got that far without being seen, I was doing all right.

I stood there a few minutes, waiting to be sure that I was still doing all right, and to let my eyes get used to the darkness. Or the not-quite-darkness; there was just a touch of gray to the sky already.

When I could see fairly well, I started moving. I decided to pick a window in about the middle of the building because there I'd be farthest from any residence where some light sleeper or insomniac might hear glass breaking if I had to break glass.

But I didn't get all the way to the middle of the building and I didn't have to break glass. God loved me. Someone had been careless; there was a window open, wide open.

I lowered myself through it and waited another few minutes—I don't know why—and then, shielding the pencil flashlight with my hand, I found my way across a classroom and into the corridor. I knew my way. Around one turn and up the middle stairs and right across from it were the offices.

The file cabinets were still in the same place. At a distance and angle from the windows and around a corner from them so I could use my flashlight, with reasonable care, without a chance of its being seen from the street. I didn't know how they were arranged but I saw one drawer labeled *1953*. And since it was now only the summer of 1952 I thought the date must mean the class of 1953, which would be Obie's class. I opened it and I was right. The folders in it each bore a name, arranged alphabetically. And among the W's I found a folder labeled *Westphal, Henry O.* I took it back into the far corner, still safer from the windows, and opened it on the floor. I had his schedules for the three years he'd attended the school, his grades and his credits, his attendance record and a few other things that weren't important from my point of view. I got the information I wanted except that there wasn't in the file any record of extracurricular activities such as membership in school clubs. Then I remembered that would be covered in the school annuals and that there was—or had been—a neat chronological row of them in the bookcase on the opposite side of the room. I put Obie's file back in the cabinet and closed the drawer.

And then went to where the bookcase was. Or used to be. It had been moved to another wall but I found it and I found the 1952 volume of the school annual. I found the pages, two of them, devoted to the Drama Club and studied them. I put the volume back in the bookcase and left the way I had come.

The sky was definitely gray now.

I was a block away from the school when the squad car passed me, being driven slowly. Two men in it. The one on my side, not the driver, looked me over as it went by but I must have looked all right, even for a five o'clock in the morning pedestrian, for the car kept on going.

But half a block farther on it pulled in to the curb in front of the car I'd left parked there. My ancient Buick. I had to keep on walking; I'd been seen and if I turned around and started the other way they'd have been stupid not to pick me up for questioning. So I kept on going toward the Buick, and the crowbar that I hadn't had to use banged against my leg at every step.

One of the two policemen was still in the squad car parked just ahead. The other had his foot on my front bumper and was writing out a ticket. He looked up from his writing as I came close. "Your car?"

I nodded.

He said, "The whole Goddam block to park in, nothing else near, and you park in front of a fireplug. Been drinking, pal?"

I looked and I *had* parked in front of a fireplug. It was so ridiculous that I wanted to laugh and, for the moment, I quit being scared. I said, "No, I haven't been drinking. But my parking there sure must look as though I had been. My God, I deserve a ticket for that one."

I should have argued; I should have realized that it makes a cop suspicious if you don't argue with him.

He looked at me. "Where you been, this time of night?"

The other cop was getting out of the car now, coming to join the first one. The crowbar hanging down my right trouser leg felt as though it weighed a ton and must be noticeable a mile away. But my mind was still working.

I said, "Visiting a friend," and had the rest of my story planned.

"We passed you walking almost a block back. Where does your friend live? How come you didn't park in front of his house?"

I took a deep breath and let it out as though I was trying to decide whether to tell him something or not. Then I said, "I parked over a block away on purpose, Officer. And for the same reason that I'm leaving at this hour, before her neighbors might be awake and see me."

"Let's see your license."

I reached for it thankfully. If they were going to pat me over for a gun—and find that damned crowbar— they'd have done it before they let me reach into a pocket for my wallet. I was okay now; I could show them I was a solid citizen and not a burglar. That crowbar would have been something to explain. I handed them my wallet, opened out, instead of slipping the driver's license out of it; that way they could see the license under the celluloid window on one side and my press pass under the window on the other.

The cop who'd just got out of the car looked over the other's shoulder. He said, "Reporter. What the hell, Hank, he'll just square a ticket if you give him one. Come on."

"Not this time," I said. "Think I want to tell Joe Steiner I parked in front of a fireplug in an empty block at night? And have him kid me about it for the next year? This one I'll pay, if you give me a ticket."

The first cop put his foot on the bumper again, ready to write. He said, "Okay, if you want one."

The second one said, "Ahh, nuts. Give the guy a break. He had hot pants when he parked there. His mind wasn't on fireplugs."

The first cop took his foot off the bumper and put the pad in his pocket. He said, "Okay, okay. Next time *look*, though."

I said, "Thanks, boys. How's about telling me your names? So if they ever pop up in a story I'll at least see that they're spelled right."

They told me their names and how to spell them and we talked a few minutes. Then they got in the squad car and drove off.

I got behind the wheel of the Buick, turned on the lights and started the engine, and then decided to sit there and jitter a minute before I started driving. I got the crowbar out and reached over and put it on the floor in the back seat. I never wanted to see a crowbar again in my life.

And how damned lucky it was that I hadn't had to use it to break in! If I'd had to jimmy a window there'd be a burglary report made tomorrow by the high school. And since this was their beat those squad cops would get the report and, solid citizen though they now thought me, they'd remember the hour of my return to my car and want to ask me some more questions. Oh, I could have bluffed it through, even with Chief Steiner, by sticking to my story and refusing to divulge the name of my mythical friend to give myself an alibi. But it wouldn't have helped my standing with the police department. As things had worked out, though, I felt sure that I'd left everything at the school just as I'd found it and that there wouldn't be any report of a burglary.

I drove home because there wasn't any other place to go. I wanted a drink badly, several drinks. But there wasn't anything to drink at home and where can you get a drink or a bottle at five o'clock? Of course I could commit another burglary, a liquor store this time. But not right now, thanks. Some other time, not right now.

It was getting light by the time I got home.

Well, I'd found out what I wanted to know, and without having to confide in Nina so she'd get the information for me. The file on Obie plus the annual for the last year had given me the three facts I wanted. And I wished now that they had been otherwise. If I could have given Obie an alibi for, say, two out of the three deaths that he might have caused at the school, I might have been able to write off the whole thing and forget it. But things hadn't been that simple for me.

In his freshman year Obie had had a fifth-period algebra class; that meant his lunch period was the second one. He could have pushed Wilbur Greenough from the tower window. He had been in the same gym class as the Negro boy who'd been killed in the gym locker room.

And he'd belonged to the Drama Club. In fact, he must have been a very active member of it because the two pages of the school annual of last year given to the Drama Club had shown scenes from and listed the cast of the three plays the Drama Club had put on. Obie had played the lead in one and a supporting role in each of the others. There was every chance that Obie had attended the meeting that preceded the death of Constance Bonner and had known that she was alone in the school building after it.

I'd noticed too that one of the three plays had been Shakespeare's *Othello* and that Obie had played the role of Iago. Iago, murderer. Iago, almost the only villain in literature who knew he was a villain and gloried secretly in his villainy and his cleverness in concealing it. Had Obie *chosen* that role?

I'd glanced back in the faculty section of the annual too and had looked at the picture of Constance Bonner. With a light tasteful black border around it and the date of her death. Just "Died, January 24, 1952"; whether accident, suicide or murder not specified.

So Obie could have killed all three of them.

All right, Sam Evans, what now? Where do you go from here?

· 2 ·

Five-thirty in the morning is a hell of a time for it to be unless you're sleepy or unless you've got something to do. I'd never felt wider awake in my life and there wasn't any use in my going back to bed.

There wasn't any use in my doing anything else either. Particularly there wasn't any use in my trying to think anymore about anything. Nor in trying to read to pass the time; I did try that and found I couldn't concentrate for two consecutive sentences.

I wandered around like a lost soul for a while and then decided I might as well be doing something useful so I straightened up the house. Washed the few dishes and glasses I'd used, made the bed, did a little dusting in places where dust showed. Daylight by the time I'd finished all that. I remembered the coal bin in the basement that had broken last winter and which I had to fix some-

time before we ordered more coal in the fall. And that
sometime had might as well be now. I started to change
into old clothes for the job and then decided what the
hell, why get even old clothes full of coal dust? I went
down to the basement wearing only a pair of shoes, the
ideal costume for carpentering a coal bin. It was a lot
bigger job than I'd thought; I didn't finish until almost
ten o'clock. I took off the worst of the dirt at the faucet
in the basement and then went upstairs to the bathroom
and shaved while I drew a full tub of hot water.

I got in and it felt good. I made myself comfortable
with my head on the end of the tub and the next thing I
knew the water was cold and twelve o'clock whistles
were blowing. I dried myself and dressed. I could have
gone to bed instead and slept a few more hours except
that I was ravenously hungry and there was nothing in
the house.

I went to a good restaurant and ate a big meal. When
I came out it was a bright afternoon and I had a bright
idea. There's a small privately owned lake only twelve
miles from town on Highway 71 where the fishing is
fairly good and where you can rent a boat, a rod, full
fishing equipment. Why didn't I get away from everything I'd been thinking about and worrying about and
have myself at least half a day's fishing? Afternoon isn't
the best time, of course, but I still might catch a few
and if I didn't it wouldn't matter too much.

I got in the Buick and headed out of town west on 71.

I was just a mile or so past the city limits when I began
to be convinced that I was being followed. By a jalopy.

I hadn't been looking for a tail, nothing had been
farther from my mind. But I'd happened to notice this
jalopy—it wasn't the topless one with the wolf's head
on the radiator; this one was a hard-topped coupe, vintage
of about 1930—while we were still back in town. I'd
noticed it because I'd come perilously close to running
a red light and I'd looked in my rear vision mirror to see

if a police car or motorcycle was coming after me. None was, but I saw that the car behind me was running the light too, taking more of a chance than I had. And it had stayed with me, dropping back to a little greater distance when we were out of town traffic, but passing cars when I passed them and yet not passing me, holding his distance behind me and not closing up, when I slowed down quite a bit to see what he'd do.

He was good at it. I'd probably never have noticed him if it hadn't been for what had happened at the stop light.

It scared me a little. Obie? Apparently he didn't have a car of his own, but he could have borrowed one from a friend—and the jalopy following me was the kind of car a high school kid would be likely to have. But why would Obie be following *me*? I thought back and couldn't figure any way in which he could have learned that I was interested in him. I hadn't asked many people questions about him and none of the people I'd even mentioned his name to had been close to him or likely to tell him about it.

Dr. Wygand? I'd come nearer to talking frankly to him than to anyone else but it was ridiculous to think he'd have called Obie or even Armin Westphal to say I'd been asking questions. Doc is a right guy. The only person I'd talked to about Obie who could have felt close to him was Grace Smith, his classmate, but that had been while she and I and everyone else had thought Obie had been killed by the roller coaster and my questions had been the legitimate questions of a reporter at work. No, that was out.

But who else would be following me in a jalopy? Police or private detectives don't use conspicuously ancient wrecks like that one for tailing.

All I could tell at the distance it kept behind me was that there was only one person, the driver, in it.

Did I have nerve enough to force the issue and find

out who he was? I decided that I did but that I'd rather do it in a town, where there'd be other people around, than out here on the open road. Barnesville, a town with a wide main street, good for making U-turns, was only a mile or two ahead and I'd do it there. I drove at an even speed and the jalopy kept an even distance behind me. It dropped back a little when we entered the town.

I made my play when we were a little way into Barnesville but not yet to the business section. I went to one side of the street and drove along slowly and pretended to be watching street numbers. I made a point of not looking back but the jalopy didn't pass me.

I stopped in front of a house and got out. I managed to glance back without seeming to do it deliberately as I closed the door of the car. The jalopy was parking about half a block behind me. Still too far for me to see the driver or read the license plate.

I did what I thought was a nice bit of acting, a double take on the house number, as though I'd read it wrong the first time. I made a pass at going back to my car and then pretended to decide that there was no use moving it and that I'd walk back to the right number. I started walking briskly back toward the jalopy, pretending to watch the house numbers to my left but able, since it was in the general direction I was walking, to keep a watch on the jalopy too. I figured that by the time he could do anything I'd be close enough to get a look at him and to read the license plate.

But maybe my acting hadn't been so hot or maybe he was smarter than I'd given him credit for being. Apparently he'd kept his engine running and I hadn't taken more than a dozen steps before he shoved his car into gear and got the hell out of there. He U-turned right from the curb and headed back the way we'd come.

He must have had a good lead on me by the time I got back to my car and got it started; *I* hadn't been smart enough to leave the engine running. And a stream of traffic materialized and kept me from U-turning for another minute or two—and that was too long. I drove back to town as fast as I dared but I never caught him. Maybe he'd played safe by turning off just outside Barnesville somewhere. Or maybe the jalopy was a hot rod and he'd simply walked away from me.

Well, there was one thing I could do, anyway. Find out whether Obie was home. I parked and went into a drugstore, used the phone booth to call the Westphal residence. A female voice answered and I asked if Obie was there.

"Just a moment, please."

I wanted to be sure; she might think he was somewhere around when he wasn't. But a minute later Obie's voice said, "Hello." I recognized the voice; I'd heard him talking to his friends in the railroad station a couple of days ago. But he'd never heard my voice and I didn't want him to. Nor the click of a phone being hung up on him. I just waited until he'd said "Hello" a few more times and then replaced the receiver on his end.

It hadn't been Obie in the jalopy that had followed me. His home was on another side of town, a good five miles from here. And the jalopy couldn't possibly have done ten miles while I'd chased it five, not unless it had averaged over a hundred and twenty miles an hour for ten miles, five miles of which was on city streets. And that was ridiculous.

I drove back out on Highway 71 and spent the afternoon fishing at the private lake but I didn't enjoy it very much. I kept wondering and worrying about that jalopy. I tried to tell myself I might have been mistaken about it and that its U-turn and getaway just when I was walking back to it had been coincidence. But I knew damned well it hadn't been.

I caught three pike but when I stopped home to dress

for dinner with Nina I gave them to a neighbor. If I'd
taken them with me to Nina's she might have insisted
on cooking them for us and I'd decided definitely that I
wanted to take her out this evening and didn't want any
argument about it.

No car, jalopy or other, followed me between home
and Nina's. I made sure of that because if whoever had
followed me before wanted to pick me up again he'd
have been waiting somewhere near my house to do it.

· 3 ·

I got there a few minutes early but, miraculously, Nina
was ready. She was beautiful in a white silk dinner dress
that fitted her like a coat of paint and set off her slightly
olive skin and dark hair and eyes.

I kissed her and it was as though I hadn't kissed her
for weeks and had been missing her every minute. Her
lips were hungry against mine and she clung to me. Then
she put her head back but kept her arms around me and
looked at me, her eyes a little misty.

"I'm so glad you came tonight, Sam."

"I am too, darling."

"There isn't much more time, is there?"

I knew what she meant and I wanted suddenly to tell
her there was all the time in the world and that I loved
her to pieces. But I didn't know for sure whether that
was true or not and so I couldn't say it.

"I don't know," I had to say. "All I know is that
right now I love you."

She smiled. "Thanks for that, anyway. And I'm sorry—
I didn't mean to sound so serious. It's been wonderful."

"It's still wonderful," I told her. "Don't make it

sound like a valedictory.'' But I was thinking: This is Friday evening. Millie will probably be home the day after tomorrow. And what will happen then?

I knew one thing that wouldn't happen. I wouldn't live with Millie and keep on seeing Nina, clandestinely. There'd have to be a clean break one way or the other.

Nina stepped back from me. ''Let's have one drink here before we leave. Like a Martini?''

''I'd love a Martini.''

''As much as you love me?'' Her tone was light.

''At least as much.''

''Good. You break out the ice cubes while I get the rest of the things.''

The Martinis were excellent. We sat together on the sofa to drink them and my arm went about her as naturally as though it belonged there, which it did. And you need only one hand to drink a cocktail; not always even that if there's a coffee table in front of you to put it down on.

After we'd finished our drinks I drove us out to the Club Caesar. It's small and pretty expensive, I'd heard. But I could stand the expense for one evening and the expensiveness had one advantage; there was little likelihood that anyone I knew would be there. And no one was.

We each had another cocktail and then a good dinner, a damn good dinner. T-bone steaks, if it matters. It did matter then because I was starving by the time the steaks came.

After dinner we danced, and not to a blaring orchestra but to music made by one man on one piano. A good man, a good piano, and good music. Music that you could talk against easily when you wanted to sit at your table and talk, as we did about half of the time. I've often wondered why the less you pay at a place the more music you get, in volume.

We talked about her jobs, the school one and the social service one, about my job, about old times—our classes at high school and our teachers—and Nina could tell me which ones of them were still teaching there—and it was as though Nina and I hadn't until then really got around to talking much. And somehow we seemed closer to one another than we'd ever been before—even in bed.

After a while Nina said, "Let's go back to my place, Sam. We can have a nightcap there."

I looked at my watch. "It's early, only eleven. And tomorrow's Saturday. No school."

"I've got to get up early just the same. My other job—I've got a nine o'clock appointment."

"All right," I said. "If you won't kick me out too soon after we get to your place. You had a good night's sleep last night. Or did you?"

"Ten hours, yes. Did you get to bed early?"

"Eleven o'clock." I didn't add that I'd slept only about three hours then and another hour or so in the bathtub at around noon.

"Good. Oh—what was it you wanted to talk to me about last night, Sam? Sorry I didn't feel up to letting you come around, by the way."

"Nothing important," I said. Then I remembered I'd said last night that it *was* important. "Something I wanted you to find out for me from the school files. But I got the information myself." And then I realized what I'd said and added quickly, "Today, from the newspaper files." Damn, that had been a silly thing to say. I thought that I'd covered all my tracks at the high school last night, but if I hadn't, if Nina knew that the offices there had been entered last night, I was giving myself away.

But apparently everything was all right. She asked, "Something in connection with your article on accidents?" And I nodded and she let it go at that and I didn't have to think up any further evasions.

I called for the check and it wasn't as stiff as I'd expected.

Driving back, I watched closely for headlights that

might be following me, but there weren't any. Once in town I took a route that used little frequented streets and for blocks at a time there wasn't any other car in sight.

We made Martinis again. We were getting to be a good team at it. Fast and efficient, each of us having his allotted part in the operation. It just couldn't be, I thought, that this was the last or almost the last time we'd make them together.

And again we sat on the sofa with my arm around her and I felt at peace and unworried. Which worried me. It's one thing when a married man feels excited about a woman other than his wife; he can get over that. But when he feels at peace with her, it's serious.

And suddenly I wanted to level with Nina. Not about our personal relationships, not about that until I was sure and it would be wrong for me to be sure until after I'd seen Millie again. I mean about what I'd really been investigating, or trying to investigate, this week. About Obie, and what I thought he was. It was something I'd have to talk over with someone, sometime, if only to see how it sounded when put in words. And would she laugh at me or take it seriously?

"Nina, how well do you know Obie Westphal? What do you think of him?"

She pulled away far enough so she could turn and look at me and there was surprise in her face. "Sam, why on earth are you interested in Obie Westphal? You asked me questions about him earlier this week."

I thought, not yet; tell her in a minute but first get an unbiased opinion, what she thinks of him now before I tell her anything. Or maybe evasion had become a habit by now, too strong to break suddenly. I said, "I told you why I was interested, then. I spent last Saturday morning working on him, writing an obituary, a sob story, before it was known that the boy who was killed was Jimmy Chojnacki and not Obie. I read about him, what there was in our files, and I talked about him to one of his classmates who had a crush on him, and I wrote about him. I got interested in him, say, like you get interested in a character in a book." I took a sip of the drink in my free hand and pulled Nina back against me with the other. "Only with a character in a book all you can ever learn about him is what's in the book. But Obie's not only real, he's still alive after I wrote an obit on him. So why would it be strange that I'm interested in him."

Why, I wondered, had I gone that far, been that elaborate. Now, if I leveled with her, it was going to be tougher to explain and I'd have to admit that I'd lied to her just now as well as earlier in the week.

Nina put her head on my shoulder. "Well, I don't know him personally except just to speak to. But he's so popular, so prominent at the school that the teachers talk about him a lot, almost as much as the students. Of course being a football hero is enough, in a school. But being so personally attractive and such a brilliant student besides being an athletic hero—well, it makes him pretty unusual."

"Just how brilliant a student is he? Leads his class?"

"I think he easily could if he wanted to. His average is in the top ten per cent, and that's without studying very hard. He can't put in much time on studying with all the other activities and athletics he goes in for. And he admits he doesn't study much."

I said, "A high school boy doesn't admit that, he brags about it. But here's what I'm really digging for. He's too good to be true; there's got to be a flaw, a fault somewhere, or I just can't believe him. Nobody's perfect, and one boy can't have just everything. I think he's queer."

"You think—*what?*"

"All right, it's a guess. But there's something to base it on anyway. Grace Smith—that's the classmate of his I talked to Saturday morning while we thought he was dead, and she was all broken up about it, incidentally— said he not only didn't have a steady girl, but usually went stag to parties. And—'' I started to say that the time I'd seen him in the wolf's-head jalopy the two other boys had had girls and Obie hadn't, but I changed it. ''—I've heard the same thing from other places. It isn't normal, is it, for a boy with a whole school full of girls mad over him not to take advantage of some of it. Especially one as well developed and mature for his age as Obie. If he isn't queer, then he's sexually retarded.''

''But at seventeen, Sam, you hadn't— At least you told me I was the first, and that was in our senior year and we were both eighteen then.''

''True, and I wasn't kidding you. But dammit I *went* with girls, dated 'em, long before then. Generally I was going steady with someone, and I never stagged a party in my life.''

Nina's shoulder, against mine, was shaking. I turned and looked at her; she was giggling. ''What's funny about that?'' I wanted to know. ''You know it's perfectly true.''

''I wasn't laughing about that, Sam, not about what you said about yourself. But—Sam, if I tell you something that's a secret, will you promise never to— You're not planning to *write* anything about Obie, are you?''

''Nope.''

''And you won't tell this to anyone? Word of honor?''

''Cross my heart and hope to die.''

''I was laughing at how *wrong* you were about Obie. A little over a year ago, near the end of his sophomore year, he got into a little trouble for seducing a maid they had working for them at the house, the Westphal home. And he'd have been only sixteen then; he beat your record by two years. That's what I was giggling about. Your thinking he was queer.''

''So I was wrong. I've been wrong before. Who was

he in trouble with? And how did the school get in on it if it's something that happened at home?''

"I didn't mean trouble really, except with his parents. The girl didn't go to the police or anything like that—and anyway she probably seduced him; she was older. But Mama Westphal was so worried about it that she came to the principal of the school for advice.''

"Old Emerson? Must have shocked the bejesus out of him. What did he tell her?''

"It wasn't Mr. Emerson. Probably luckily for every-body concerned. He's still principal there, Sam, but he was out for a few months right about then, in the hospital for an operation—gall bladder trouble; he was quite ill for a while. The school board sent us a younger man, Ralph Sherbourne, to take over during those months. Mama Westphal talked to him about it and he was modern and sensible enough to tell her it was nothing to worry about. That while he didn't condone it, there was nothing abnormal about a boy of sixteen having his first affair with an older woman.''

I thought of Constance Bonner. I asked, "How much older?''

"I believe she was twenty-five or thereabouts. And there was a question whether she seduced Obie or he seduced her, and it wasn't anything serious anyway.''

I said, "And Obie at sixteen was probably a couple of years ahead of his age in physical development. Right now at seventeen he could probably pass for twenty, somebody told me. But go on, if there's any more you know about it. I'm interested.''

"There isn't much more. Ralph calmed down Mama Westphal and told her he'd have a heart-to-heart talk with Obie. And he did and Obie was sorry about it and promised to behave himself.''

"Did you ever see the girl, the maid? Or a picture of her?''

"Of course not. Where would I see her? Why do you ask that, Sam?"

"Wondering something. Oedipus. The girl was probably the same physical type as Obie's mother."

"Maybe. I suppose it could be that. I've never seen Obie's mother either. I wasn't there the day she came in. But if Obie takes after her, she must be good-looking. Have you ever seen Obie, Sam?"

"No," I said. "Just a picture of him in football costume that was in the file on him at the *Herald*, along with the sports stories we'd run on him. And you can't tell much from a picture of somebody in football clothes and helmet."

"I've got a copy of last year's school annual," Nina said. "There are several pictures of him in it. Want to see them?"

I'd seen them last night at the school, or at least the ones in the Drama Club section, but I couldn't very well say so now. So I said yes, I'd like to see them.

She had only to lean forward to get the annual. It was on the bottom shelf of the coffee table in front of us, with some magazines and other books.

"Our drinks are gone," I said. "Let's make another before we look at that. He's probably in it a dozen times and it'll take a little while to leaf through it."

"All right, but this one had better be our last. I'm feeling them."

"Good. Glad they're not being wasted. I'm feeling mine too."

We made us each another drink.

Then I watched while Nina leafed through the book, stopping whenever there was a group photograph that included Obie—and he was in quite a few of them. He stood out in every group, too; you couldn't miss him. I saw again the three group pictures of Drama Club casts that included Obie.

I asked Nina, "Is he as good at acting as at everything else?"

"Good for an amateur. I saw all of those plays, as it happens."

The last picture of Obie in the book was the best one I'd seen yet, an eighth-page portrait shot among the pictures of class officers.

Nina closed the book and put it back under the coffee table.

"Nina," I said, "how many people know what you told me about Mrs. Westphal's asking for advice about Obie's affair with that girl? Is it general knowledge among the teachers there?"

"Why—no, Sam." She moved away from me a little. "Aside from Ralph Sherbourne, I'm the only one at the school who knew about it. He told me later. And you'll guess why he happened to talk about it to me, so I might as well tell you. Do I have to add anything to that, spell it out for you?"

I pulled her back against me again, both arms around her this time. I said, "Of course not. It's none of my business, Nina."

She snuggled against me. "I told you I'd had affairs, a few of them. And Ralph was one of those few. And he was single and wanted me to marry him. Maybe I should have, but—well, he's a nice guy but I just didn't love him enough to sign a life contract. Damn it, Sam, maybe the only men I can really love are ones I can't have. Do you still want to kiss me, Sam?"

I answered without words. After a while she pulled away gently just enough to free her lips for talking. "Sam, I shouldn't, but I'll have one more drink if you will. I guess I slept too much last night; I just can't get tired."

We made the drinks and this time I sat in the easy chair and pulled her down into my lap.

After a while I said, "Darling, must I go home tonight?

It's so damned lonesome there and I hate it. I didn't sleep much last night in spite of going to bed early. Can I sleep with you, even if I have to behave myself?''

She turned her head so I could see her smile. ''Will you wear a pair of my pajamas?''

''I will not. But you can. And I'll sleep in my shorts. That's two layers of insulation.''

''All right, Sam, yes, I want you to stay.''

Later, in bed, I held her tightly.

''Do you think I'm a wanton woman, Sam?''

''Of course not.''

''But I feel like one. Right now. And I'm not very sick, darling; it was mostly a false alarm. Do you want me, Sam?''

God how I'd been wanting her.

Later, I remember saying, ''Nina darling, I love you, I love you.'' Or words to that effect.

SATURDAY

·1·

I woke too early again. Not from a dream this time; if I'd been dreaming I didn't remember. Faint gray at the windows, probably about half past five, Daylight Saving Time, maybe six. Nina had set her mental alarm clock for eight, saying that would give her time for her nine o'clock appointment and that I could sleep longer if I wished and leave as late as I wanted to.

But here again after only a few hours of sleep I was wide awake and knew that I wasn't going back to sleep no matter how hard I tried. And Nina is a light sleeper; I couldn't get up without waking her too. Besides, if I did get up, what could I do?

I lay there and stared at the barely visible ceiling. No horsefly circling there. Just my thoughts again. Why hadn't I told Nina the truth last night? Just force of habit, maybe; I'd been lying so much this last week that the truth didn't come naturally any more, not in explaining my reason for asking questions about Obie. Well, it didn't matter; Nina had talked plenty about him, maybe even more freely than she would have if I'd told her my suspicions and she'd thought them ridiculous. As she no doubt would have. Apparently Obie was damned attractive even to women Nina's age. In fact—

Whoa, I told myself, don't get a wild suspicion like *that*. Not about Nina.

But there was the Suspicion sitting on the foot of the bed grinning at me, a nasty grin.

"Go away," I told it.

"How about the way she giggled when you wondered whether Obie was queer or not?"

I glared at the Suspicion. "Why shouldn't she giggle? She knew it wasn't true!"

"Right, my naïve friend. She knew it wasn't true. But would the matter have seemed so *funny* to her if she had that knowledge third hand? And Nina isn't the giggly type. In fact, you never heard her giggle before—not since high school days anyway. But if *she'd* had an affair with him and he was a pretty virile guy, as he probably is, maybe twice or three times as much so as *you* are, then your suddenly suggesting he might be homosexual would have been *really* funny to her, so much so that a giggle just had to pop out and she couldn't stop it."

"But she explained how she knew! Do you think she could make up a circumstantial story like that on a second's notice?"

"I doubt if she made it up. Probably there was such a substitute principal and he did have an affair with Nina—maybe he even really wanted to marry her, although that could have been embroidery. And probably the servant girl business and Mrs. Westphal's trip to the school really did happen. Don't you see why that makes it all the more likely?"

"No, I don't."

"Because you don't want to see. Ordinarily Nina would never have thought of having an affair with a seventeen-year-old. But after knowing that he'd already had an affair—at least one affair—with a woman approximately her age, she'd look at Obie with new eyes, wouldn't she? And she admits she found him damned attractive—and there'd have been curiosity too, wondering what he'd be like in bed. Curiosity gets women into more affairs than passion does."

I said, "You're crazy. But at least the Constance

Bonner business makes sense now. *She* must have been having an affair with Obie. And that's why she made an excuse to stay at the school after the Drama Club meeting. He came back for a clandestine date with her. Since she was living with her parents that was about the only place—''

"Nina isn't living with parents. She's got this—''

"Shut up. I'm thinking about Constance Bonner. This accounts for that part about her having been acting strangely, being depressed. If she'd become seriously entangled emotionally with someone she couldn't possibly marry. . . . But Obie killed her. He didn't kill Nina. Doesn't that prove—''

"You know it doesn't. He doesn't have to kill every woman he makes. Just if a perfect opportunity pops up, maybe, like a woman who can't swim standing at the edge of the deep end of a swimming pool where a push will kill her. Or maybe he had a sane motive for killing Constance and led her to the pool deliberately. Maybe he was through with her and she wouldn't let go and she was threatening him with something.''

"What does it matter? Anyway, you're just trying to change the subject. We were wondering about Nina and Obie, remember?''

"I still say you're crazy. Nina isn't that kind of a girl.''

"How long did it take you to make her? Met her Monday noon and slept here Monday night. And don't give me that stuff about having been sweethearts in school. That was a long time ago.''

"Nuts. And anyway, you're building an awful lot on one giggle.''

"You know there's more than that, now that you think about it. The way she talked about him, described him. The fact that she has that school annual with all the pictures of him—and knew where they were. She hasn't got school annuals for other years since you and she were students there, has she? Just that one, and it's got a lot of pictures of Obie in it. Don't you think she might have bought it for that reason?"

"There could be other reasons," I said.

"Name one. And that annual is only two months or so off the presses, by the way. Her affair with Obie could have been quite recent. How do you like *that* thought? Obie may have been in this bed with her within a month or so. Maybe they just broke it off before you met her— and you got her on the rebound. From *Obie*. Isn't that nice to think about?"

"Get out. Get away from me."

"You know I never will, until you know for sure one way or the other. I'll be with you all my life."

"But I won't believe you."

"Of course you won't, but you'll always wonder. And you'll keep remembering other little things. She called Mrs. Westphal *Mama* Westphal, a kind of humorous deprecation, although she never met her. Where'd she pick that up, huh? She saw all of the plays of the Drama Club that Obie played in last year. Adults seldom go to high school plays unless they have relatives in the cast— or something."

"But she *works* there."

"Yeah, yeah. Plenty of chance to come in contact with him. And remember our figuring out this Oedipus stuff? That means Obie would pick women of the same general physical type as his mother, ones who remind him of her in some way. And Nina's the size and build for that, same color hair, same shaped face. Same general type as the Bonner woman, too, as far as you could tell from a portrait photograph. Never thought of that till just now, did you? And you'll keep thinking of other little things and—"

I said, "Get out."

The Suspicion laughed at me.

I turned my head and looked at Nina.

The Suspicion said, "Go ahead and wake her up, make love to her. And if she happens to close her eyes while it's going on, as she usually does, you'll wonder whether she's pretending that it's Obie again instead of only you. Some fun, huh?"

I swore. I said, "You *won't* get me to do what you want me to do. Those journals of Nina's—"

"It would be a lousy trick to look in them, sure. Even if you just skimmed, looking for one thing, and tried not to read or remember anything else. But you're going to do it."

"Are you sure of that?"

"Sure I'm sure. Because now that you've got *me* it'll be an even dirtier trick if you don't. Because that's the only way you can ever get rid of me and you know it. Do you love Nina?"

"I—don't—know."

"Last night you thought you did. You told her you did. But you never can love her again unless you find out I'm wrong. And is it fair to Nina for you to change toward her because of a nasty Suspicion like me, when you can get rid of me forever by skimming through one or two of those diaries?"

"But what if I can't find—?"

"Don't worry, you'll find it if it's there. If there's anything at all about Obie there'll be plenty about him and it won't be hard to find even if she disguises the name. And you can love her in spite of anything *else* you might find there. You don't care how many *normal* affairs she'd had in the last year or so. And you can skip this last week and not read anything she may have written about *you*."

"All right, damn you."

"Just play possum now. It must be almost time for—"

Nina woke and got out of bed. I played possum all right; as long as I did so that Suspicion sitting on the end of the bed would be invisible to Nina. If I talked to her she might see it, or at least guess that something was wrong.

So I kept my eyes closed and didn't move except to breathe while I heard her shower and dress, make herself breakfast and make a scratching noise with a pen that I guessed meant she was leaving a note for me.

After the door closed I looked at the clock and decided I'd stay as I was another ten minutes so I could still pretend to be asleep if she came back for a purse or a coat or a handkerchief. But she didn't. I got up and read the note first

Dearest: I'll not work long today. My nine o'clock appointment will take me at least an hour but maybe I'll make that my only call of the day and come home right after. If I make another call or two they'll be short; I'll be back between half past ten and eleven o'clock. If you're up sooner than that, why not make yourself some breakfast here and wait for me? I can make us a picnic lunch and we can go somewhere out in the country and have a wonderful quiet Saturday afternoon together. And I won't hold you to what you said last night, but I'd love to hear you say it again. Or was it the Martinis talking? If it was, I'll forgive you.

Nina

Yes, it made me feel ashamed of myself, that note. But I still had to do what I was going to do. And it wasn't quite nine o'clock now so I had an hour and a half to do it in. An hour, to give myself a big factor of safety.

I dressed quickly.

The lock on the desk drawer in which Nina kept her

journals looked as though it would open with a hairpin but it would be easier and better if I could find where Nina kept the key to it. I tried to remember where she'd taken the key from and where she'd put it afterwards, the night she'd opened that drawer to get me data on the accidents at the school. No, I'd been making drinks and hadn't seen her get the key or open the drawer, but afterwards she locked the drawer again and put the key in the pocket of her housecoat. A quilted silk one.

I found the housecoat among her clothes in the closet, but of course the key wasn't in its pocket. That would have been a temporary repository until she could put it in its usual place while I wasn't watching.

I tried the unlocked drawers of the desk itself first; it wasn't there. But my second guess, the dresser, was right. It was under the paper lining the bottom of the drawer. A minute later I was on the sofa with the current volume of Nina's journal.

I leafed through the blank pages quickly until I found the most recent entry, dated *July 17, 9:15* P.M. That would be Thursday evening, two days ago, just after I'd phoned Nina. There was about a page of it beginning: "*S. just called and wanted to come over. Wanted him to, but I'm too awfully tired, too much in need of a full night's sleep and if he comes over I know what will happen. I'll turn in as soon as I finish this . . .*"

I managed to stop there, remembering that I'd resolved not to invade Nina's privacy any more than I absolutely had to and that what she might have written about me wasn't any of my business.

I leafed back a full week to the pre-Sam period, reading only the dates of the three entries, two short and one several pages long, she'd made during that week. I managed not to read them but couldn't help noticing that my initial occurred frequently in the long entry, which was dated Tuesday afternoon, the day after the night I'd first

slept here. I'd have given a lot to read that entry but my
conscience wouldn't let me.

I skimmed rapidly over entries, mostly shortish ones,
for a month's time, averaging two or three entries a week,
and mostly things about her social service work. Names
were either written out in full or abbreviated for con-
venience rather than disguise; I saw *Anna Choj.* several
times. Apparently Nina used initials only for entries concerning matters clandestine. Knowing that let me leaf
more quickly through the next few weeks, back into May.

An entry dated *May 20* stopped me because it didn't
seem to contain any names or even initials. I started
skimming it and then found myself reading carefully.

> *So it's been a week now and I guess I'm over the
> worst of it. But I'm glad that it happened; it was
> the most wonderful experience, the most wonderful
> month, of my life. Yes, right or wrong, I'm glad it
> happened. And of course I knew that it couldn't
> last. Too, it was such a terrible risk; if it were even
> suspected. I'd have lost my job, both my jobs. And
> probably have had to move away to another city
> and start over again; it would have been terrible.
> And yet, oh God, I just couldn't help myself. . . .*

There was a cold feeling in the pit of my stomach. I
didn't finish it. I jerked back a dozen pages at once.
May 7, 4 A.M.

> *Again O. came just after midnight; he left a few
> minutes ago. I love him, I love him, and I mustn't
> let myself love him. I must keep this just a physical
> affair to me as I know it is to him. But how can I?
> God, the last four hours. He is superb; he is every-
> thing a woman dreams of. Five times and the last
> time ending only minutes ago, must have lasted well
> over an hour; I nearly went insane with ecstasy. I
> must be mad to . . .*

I heard the door opening and turned; Nina stood there smiling. Whatever was in my face as I looked at her she didn't notice at first. "Sam darling, Mr. Wolfram was called away suddenly just as we started to talk and I thought since that was off I'd come right home and we could—"

Then she must have seen my face, really seen it, for the first time. Then the book I was still holding open and the open drawer of the desk.

She did it the way that was best for both of us; I'll give her that. She turned white with anger. She came around and jerked the book out of my hand and threw it; then she slapped my face again and again with force that rocked my head and hurt me almost as much as I was already hurt inside in another way. And monotonously in a low voice she was calling me things and using words that I'd never heard a woman use before.

And there wasn't anything I could say or wanted to say even if she'd have given me the opportunity. And then, I don't know exactly how I got there and it doesn't matter, I was outside the closed door, in the hallway. I still hadn't spoken.

I walked downstairs and around the corner to my car.

· 2 ·

Home felt different. It felt like home, empty as it was, something I had come *back* to instead of fleeing from. Just the familiarity of it threw things into better perspective. A lot of things.

I could see my affair now with Nina for what it had been—an affair and nothing more. A very pleasant affair while it had lasted. And I could have wished it to end differently, but at least that ending had been final, for both of us.

I found that I didn't hate her, either; I felt sorry for her. But just the same I never wanted to see her again, however casually. Even if she ever wanted to see me again—and she wouldn't—and even if this was the end of the road between Millie and me, I could never again want to kiss her or touch her.

And I'd never forget that giggle and what had prompted it.

What now, though, about Obie? Not about his amours; they were very definitely no concern of mine. But about the murders, the killings. I hadn't anything besides my hunch and my suspicions, of course, not a shred of concrete evidence. But with those suspicions so strong and with every fact I'd been able to learn seeming to corroborate them, did I have the moral *right* to drop the matter now and forget it?

No, I didn't. But there was a simple answer that would free me. When I'd started this it had been a hunch built on a few flimsy indications. Maybe they were still flimsy but now I had a lot of indications. Enough to go to Chief of Police Joe Steiner with. I could tell him everything—well, almost everything—that I'd learned.

And then it would be up to him and I'd be out from under. Even if he laughed at me, I'd be out from under. And maybe he wouldn't laugh. I could put the case, now, so it would sound strong enough to make him want to dig a little even if only to prove to me that I was wrong.

But not today. I still felt too lousy about Nina to want to do anything about it today. And my mind felt a bit foggy, too, and I wanted it clear when I talked to Steiner, so I wouldn't miss any points.

I killed some time doing housework again and when it got near noon I decided that, since I'd be eating some meals here from now on even if Millie didn't return right away, I might as well restock the larder and have food on hand. I made a shopping trip to the nearest supermarket.

Getting myself a lunch and eating it and washing the dishes from it lasted me until two o'clock and at two o'clock the phone rang. It was Harvey Whelan. "You all right, Sam?"

"In the pink," I told him.

"Uh—whatever it was you went back to town for, it's all okay? You got it under control?"

"Absolutely."

"Good. We got back a little sooner than we'd planned, too. Last night. Got tired of playing cards two-handed. And we're going to have a Saturday afternoon poker game, two-bit limit, seven-handed if you come; we got four others already."

"Swell. I'll be there. How soon?"

"Come on as soon as you can. Five of us are starting now. We called you twice about an hour ago, Sam, but you weren't in."

"Out shopping. Okay, be there in half an hour."

The game didn't break up till almost midnight and I cashed out forty-two bucks to the good.

SUNDAY

· 1 ·

The alarm clock wakened me and it was still the middle of the night, still completely dark, only when I reached out and pushed the button that should have stopped it, it didn't stop. It kept on ringing. Not steadily; it stopped a few seconds every once in a while and then started again. And in the few seconds of silence I could tell that the alarm clock in my hand, an electric one, wasn't even humming, wasn't running at all. The luminous hands stood at five minutes past three. And it wasn't the telephone; the telephone sounded different. The doorbell. Someone was ringing my doorbell at five minutes after three only maybe it wasn't five minutes after three because the clock wasn't running. But anyway it was the middle of the night and somebody was ringing the doorbell. I got my feet out of bed onto the floor and by that time I was thinking a little bit, but not much. I was thinking, as I started groping my way across the room toward the light switch, that Millie had come home on a train that got her back in the middle of the night, and then I remembered that Millie has her own key and wouldn't ring the doorbell. So it had to be a telegram, a telegram in the middle of the night, and a telegram in the middle of the night is bad news always, at least until you read it, somebody dead, and the only person I'd be sent a telegram about in the middle of the night was Millie and Millie must be dead or anyway hurt, an auto

accident, sudden sickness, and the bell downstairs ringing, ringing, ringing and I couldn't find the light switch.
And then my fingers found the switch and clicked it and
nothing happened, nothing at all, no light came on and
the doorbell kept ringing, ringing, still ringing as I groped
my way across from the useless light switch to the hallway door and through the door to the blacker blackness
of the hallway, a blackness almost tangible engulfing
me, holding me back, and I had to hurry, hurry, hurry
before the telegram went away and I wouldn't know what
had happened to Millie. Hurry, hurry, running my hand
along the hallway wall to guide me to the head of the
stairs. The doorbell stopped ringing, started again. Hurry.
(All of this taking time to tell but only seconds to happen.) Hurry, hurry; the doorbell not ringing any more,
the telegram going away because the man would think
by now, surely by now, that I wasn't home. My right
hand groping for the knob at the top of the banister, my
left hand still guiding along the wall, walking faster than
I dared. It was my left hand that saved me, my left hand
touching the light switch at the head of the stairs. I still
wasn't thinking coherently but I did realize that I could
go down those stairs faster if there was a light. I stopped
and flicked the switch. It clicked uselessly, as had the
one in the bedroom. But the fact that I'd stopped, or at
least slowed down, to click it saved me from going head
first down the long straight flight of stairs to the first
floor. For I was leaning slightly backward when I put
my foot forward for the first step of the stairs. My bare
toes kicked into something that was between me and the
step. Kicked hard, because I was still in a hurry to get
down there, darkness or not.

The thing I kicked went over the edge and bounced
noisily down the steps. At that, I almost lost my balance
and went after it, but my right hand found the ball of
the newel post and pushed me back; I fell, but I fell

backward and not forward headfirst down the stairs. I think I let out a yelp of pain too, for my big toe felt as though it had broken from kicking whatever object it had kicked.

Whatever I'd kicked bounced several times on the stairs and hit bottom with a thud that seemed to shake the house. The doorbell broke off in mid-ring.

And in the sudden stillness I could hear footsteps run lightly across the porch, down the walk. And a scraping sound that I couldn't quite identify, and then silence.

If I'd run immediately into the front bedroom and looked out the window, I'd probably have seen him. But I didn't; just at that moment I was still too confused to do anything. If I had any thought at all it was the thought that the man with the telegram was going away before I could catch him. Only after seconds, after I'd got to my feet again and was standing at the head of the stairs ready to try again, did it come to me that there was anything strange about what had just happened, that telegraph deliverers don't *run* away if they decide no one is home and that a telegram would be delivered to me at night only if it couldn't be telephoned and that *I* hadn't left any heavy object right at the head of the stairway.

In any case, whoever had rung the doorbell was gone; I'd missed him. And now the first and most important thing was *light*.

I hobbled back into the bedroom, taking my time now, found my trousers over the back of the chair and got matches out of the side pocket. I struck one, and there was light. I wasn't blind, at any rate.

I parlayed another match into an old flashlight that I remembered on the shelf in the closet. The batteries were weak but it was still usable.

I flashed it ahead of me and had dim light to guide me along the hallway and down the stairs.

A few feet from the bottom of them lay my portable

typewriter, half in and half out of a broken carrying case.
It had been, when I'd seen it last, only a couple of yards
from where it now lay, just inside the front door and in
its case. In messing around the house this morning, yesterday morning, I'd remembered that it was overdue for
cleaning and oiling and had put it in its case and stood
the case near the front door so I'd remember Monday to
take it to town with me when I went back to work. Well,
now the frame was probably sprung and it wouldn't need
cleaning and oiling.

But how had it got to the top of the stairs? During the
last few hours of that poker game we'd done a little
drinking but not too much; I'd been too nearly sober
when I'd got home to have carried that typewriter up the
stairs and left it standing crosswise at the edge of that
top step.

I looked out through the glass panel of the front door
and saw nothing but the porch, the yard, the sidewalk,
the street, all dimly illuminated by faint yellow light from
a street lamp half a block away. And I was still thinking
in terms of telegrams; I opened the door and looked to
see if there was a card hung on the outer knob, one of
those cards that tells you a messenger has tried to deliver
a telegram in your absence.

I looked down to be sure nothing had been pushed
under the door and I stepped out on the porch and made
sure nothing had been put into the mailbox.

Silence and an empty street.

No car had driven away after I'd heard those lightly
running footsteps; I was sure of that. But what had that
scraping noise been? And then, as I realized what that
sound *might* have been, I began for the first time to get
scared.

A bicycle left lying across the curb could have made
that sound when it was picked up, the scrape of a pedal
against cement.

I stepped back into the dark house and closed the door and then opened it again to see if the night latch was on. It was; the door was locked from the outside.

I remembered that the lights upstairs were on a different circuit from the downstairs ones and I flicked the hallway light switch by the front door. The light went on.

I went into the living room and turned on the lights there. I was awake by now, damned wide awake and damned scared. I stared at the telephone, wondering if I should phone the police.

And got a better idea. Obie, if it had been Obie, had left here not much over five minutes ago. On a bicycle it would take him at least ten minutes, maybe fifteen, to get home. Another five to get undressed and back to bed. If I phoned the Westphal home and woke up his parents and told them to look for Obie in his room— Well, he'd have some tall explaining to do. Then, too, unless they lied for him, and I doubted if both of them would, I'd have more than a guess to take to the police.

I'd forgotten the Westphal phone number but it took me only a minute to look it up and place the call. I heard the buzz that meant the phone was ringing and I waited, thinking out just what I was going to say.

But no one answered. After a while the operator's voice singsonged, "They do not answer. Shall I keep on ringing?" and I told her yes, that it was important.

But another few minutes convinced me that I'd been outsmarted. Obie would have thought of that possibility and he could easily have muffled the bell of the telephone so it couldn't have been heard upstairs, could even have wedged something between the bell and the clapper so it wouldn't ring at all. The sound of ringing that you hear while a number you call is being rung isn't really the sound of the other instrument ringing; it's a sound that originates in the switchboard circuit. It synchronizes with the ringing of the other phone but you hear it just the same even if the other phone's bell has been silenced.

And this wasn't Obie's first dead-of-night venture while his parents slept. There was proof of at least one other in Nina's diary. He'd have figured out long ago some way of being sure that no phone call would wake his parents while he was gone and lead to possible discovery of his absence from his room.

Reluctantly I put the phone back in its cradle.

The police? Too late now. If he wasn't home already, he'd be there and safely in bed, the phone unmuffled, by the time I argued them into sending a squad car to wake up respectable citizens in their own home in the middle of the night.

I was shivering, sitting there; the night had turned cool and I'd been sleeping in only shorts. I went upstairs with the dim flashlight and put on slippers and a bathrobe.

· 2 ·

Down into the basement to fix the upstairs lights. It would be a blown fuse, of course. It was and I replaced it with a new one. He wouldn't have come down here; he could have done his fuse blowing upstairs when he carried my typewriter up there; all he had to do was screw a bulb out of an upstairs hallway socket and short circuit the socket with a pocket screwdriver or something similar.

I went to the kitchen and started coffee in the percolator. Then upstairs to dress. No use trying to go back to sleep now.

And besides I was afraid to. What if he came back to try again? No, I didn't think he would, tonight. Some other time. Some other way.

A steering knuckle loosened on my car? Or what? Whatever it would be it would be something that would look like an accident, would leave no positive proof that it hadn't been. Obie killed only that way. He could easily have strangled me in my bed tonight or he could have beaten in my brains with a hammer or cut my throat with a carving knife from the kitchen. And he was enough bigger and stronger than I that I couldn't have stopped him from doing any of those things even if I'd awakened in time.

Back in the kitchen I poured myself coffee, and my hand was shaking and some coffee slopped over into the saucer. But why not? This was the first time anybody had ever tried to kill me.

And I'd never be safe again while Obie was free.

But how had he known?

I shoved that thought aside because I thought of something of immediate importance, something I had to do right away, even ahead of calling the police. In fact, calling the police could wait until I'd had time to think out a few angles so I could present them—or rather Joe Steiner personally—with a story that made sense down the line by including a way in which Obie could have known I was investigating him.

Millie. Millie came first. I had to phone her at her sister's in Rockford and tell her to stay there, not to return until I phoned her again that everything was all right. This was Sunday and she might be taking an early morning train unless I called her right away.

The call went through quickly. Millie must have wakened and come to the phone when her sister did; she came on the line right away when I asked for her.

"Millie, when are you planning to come back?"

"Today, Sam. Nine o'clock train. It'll get me there at three twenty-two. Will you meet me? I was going to phone and ask you to, if you were back from Laflamme."

It was all right then; if Millie was asking me to meet her, then things were going to be all right between us. Besides, I could tell from her voice.

I said, "Millie, don't come. You'll have to trust me and take my word for it, but I want you to stay there until I tell you it's all right to come back. It's something I can't explain over the phone."

"I don't understand, Sam. Don't you *want* me to—"

"Millie, I want you to come back more than anything on earth. I love you to hell and back," I said. And I did, too; I'd found that out only an hour before when I'd first thought the ringing of the bell meant a telegram and that a telegram meant Millie was sick or hurt. "It's nothing that concerns *us*. But it's awfully important that you stay away a little while, maybe just another day or two. And I'll tell you the whole story when I send for you. Won't you trust me until then?"

"Of course I trust you. But—are you in any danger?"

She'd come back despite me if I said yes. I said, "No, not in any danger. Trouble yes, but not any danger. And it's something I've got to straighten out before you come back. Love me, Millie?"

"Yes, I learned that, being away from you. I guess our separating for a week was a wonderful idea. But can't you give me even an idea what this is all about?"

"Honestly I can't, over the phone. But I'll promise you this; if it's going to be more than a few days I'll come there to tell you what it's about, the whole story."

"All right, Sam. Good-by, dear."

"Goodby, beloved."

For a moment, after I cradled the phone, I thought of going there, to Rockford, today. I wanted to see Millie, to tell her everything—except one thing that I'd never tell her, of course. And that one thing no longer meant anything or mattered; it had never happened.

But I must wait till after I'd talked to Joe Steiner; his

reaction to what I was going to tell him was a damned important factor in deciding how I was going to stay alive. If he took me seriously and started digging, he'd get the truth. And if Obie was a killer he'd get Obie and have him in an institution for the criminally insane before you could say Oedipus complex.

And even if Joe Steiner laughed at me and told me I was crazy, I'd be better off for having told him. I'd see to it somehow, even if I had to go to him and talk to him, that Obie knew I'd told everything I knew and suspected to the police, and that if anything happened to me from now on the police would take a dim view of its being an accident. Also I'd tell Obie that I was through, done, finished, investigating no more, that I'd been investigating him, yes, but that now I'd protected myself and done my duty as a citizen by taking my findings to the police and I was bailing out.

And I *was* bailing out. I had to, if it was ever going to be safe to let Millie come home. I'd done enough, too much, on my own; from now on it was up to Joe Steiner and I should have gone to him in the first place, no matter how nebulous my suspicions had been then. Why hadn't I? That sudden violent affair with Nina, maybe, had kept me mixed up, had kept me from thinking clearly.

Sunday morning, a good time to see him, too. Six o'clock now so I'd better wait at least a couple of hours, then I'd phone him and find out what time during the day I could have a talk with him.

At least a couple of hours to wait and that gave me time to think out, or try to think out, answers to the two loose ends my story would have otherwise.

First, who had followed me in a jalopy that afternoon, at a time when Obie had been home? I simply couldn't believe that Obie had an accomplice. Oh, I know that such things happen. Leopold and Loeb. Morey, Pell and

Royal, the three Michigan teen-agers who'd murdered the nurse; I'd recently read the series of articles about them in the *Saturday Evening Post*. Maybe, come to think of it, that was why the concept of a high school boy as a psychopathic murderer hadn't seemed too incredible to me. I hoped Chief Steiner had read those articles; if not I'd refer him to them. And there were other cases, not many but a few, in which psycho kills hadn't been solo jobs. Psychopaths, like birds of a feather, sometimes flock together; if one of them is homicidal he can lead the other or others down the bloody path of murder.

But Obie as a member, even as a leader, of a team? I just couldn't swallow it. He *had* to be a lone killer or the whole picture I'd formed didn't make sense.

I could weasel out of that one easily enough by failing to mention it to Steiner; I had a more coherent story for him without it. But that wouldn't be fair, and besides he might be able to fit it into the picture even though I couldn't. It had to fit in somewhere; it just couldn't be an irrelevant coincidence that someone had trailed me by mistake or for some reason not connected with what I'd been doing.

The other problem was just as puzzling. Why had Obie tried to kill me last night?

I didn't see how he could possibly know that I was investigating him. Doc Wygand? No, I'd have bet every cent I owned against a last week's newspaper that Doc wouldn't have told anyone that I'd asked questions about the Westphals. Doc isn't that kind of a guy. And no one else I'd talked to could remotely have guessed the nature of my interest in Obie. Except possibly—

Nina? It didn't make sense that Nina would have called or seen Obie yesterday after the parting scene between us. It didn't make sense, but it could have been. Women do funny things. Maybe for reasons of her own Nina had wanted Obie to know that I knew about the affair between them. Maybe just for an excuse to talk to him again, maybe to try to get him back for a while, even for a one-night encore. But she couldn't have told him I suspected him of murder, because she didn't know that herself.

Wait! She could have told him without knowing herself, if there'd been conversation about me. She could have mentioned my interest in him, the questions I'd asked about him, and then mentioned that I'd asked even more questions about the fatal accidents at the school. Those two things would have added up all right, to Obie. He'd have known the real reason for my interest.

Suddenly I got a picture that sickened me a little to think about. Nina phoning Obie, telling him there was something important to tell him that she couldn't say over the phone. Would he come to see her tonight so she could tell him? Obie sneaking out of his own house after his parents were asleep and spending a few hours with Nina—and why not, once more, even though the affair had ended? Learning, because they would have talked too, that I'd asked a lot of questions both about him and about the accidents. Learning too by a carefully worded question or two that my wife was out of town and that I'd be alone in the house tonight. Getting my address out of Nina's phone book, probably when she went into the bathroom. Stopping to see me on his way home.

That was the way it added up, the only way I could figure how Obie would know that I was onto him, and I hated it. I hated the thought that he had probably come here from Nina's bed. The bed I'd slept in the night before—and in which I'd told Nina that I loved her, less than thirty hours ago.

I didn't *want* to hate Nina. I tried desperately not to. I told myself that if Obie had come back to Nina when she'd called him, it meant that she had been the one who had broken off the affair originally, a month or so ago, and that her calling him back had been reaction, an act of defiance against me because I'd read her diary and learned about it. And as soon as she regained her senses she'd stop the affair again, for the reasons she'd stopped it in the first place. Thinking that made me feel a little better. Not much.

I poured myself another cup of coffee and it was the last of the pot; it would be my sixth cup since I'd made the coffee. And this time I made myself some breakfast to go with it and another pot of coffee. Daylight out now, and in an hour or so I could make my call to Steiner.

But damn oh damn, what was I going to tell him, without bringing Nina's name into it, about how Obie could have learned that I was investigating him? For a minute it had me stumped; then I felt better when I realized the question would probably never occur to him if I told him that I'd asked questions of a lot of people who knew Obie. It would seem natural that the news would get back to Obie if only I didn't stress how careful I'd been to avoid just that.

At nine o'clock on the head I phoned Steiner.

· 3 ·

A woman's voice—Mrs. Steiner's, I guessed—said, "I'm sorry. He isn't home."

"Do you know where I can reach him?"

"I'm afraid you can't today. He went on a fishing trip for the weekend."

Damn. "Do you know when he'll be back?"

"They're driving back early tomorrow morning. He's going right to the office. He'll try to be there by nine o'clock, his usual time."

Twenty-four hours to wait! I said, "This is very important. Do you happen to know *where* he's fishing? I'll drive out there, even on the off chance of finding him."

"He mentioned the river, but I don't know just where. They were going to rent a boat."

That made it hopeless. You can fish the river anywhere, either side of town for forty or fifty miles, and especially if he was out in a boat, I wouldn't find him in a week. I thanked her.

"Pardon me, but if it's police business his office is open, of course. Captain Kuehn is in charge on Sundays."

I thanked her again and hung up. There was no more use telling my story to Kuehn than in writing it in a letter to Santa Claus. Kuehn is skeptical and sarcastic, and to top it off he doesn't like me. His mind would be closed even before I started to talk. Of course if I died accidentally a week or two later, he'd remember and do something about it then, but that would be a little late to do me any good.

All right, then, I'd wait till Steiner got back, but I wasn't going to wait in this house, a sitting duck if Obie decided to try again right away. I'd spend today and tonight at a hotel downtown. Tomorrow morning I'd phone the *Herald* and tell them I'd be an hour or two late and I'd be at Steiner's office waiting for him when he showed up.

I went over the house again straightening things and closing and locking windows—there'd been two downstairs windows open so I hadn't had to wonder how Obie got in—and then I threw a few things into a bag and took off.

Before I took my car out of the garage or even turned on the ignition I raised the hood and looked things over carefully, especially what I could see of the steering mechanism. I couldn't spot anything wrong or any signs of tampering. Apparently Obie hadn't thought of that one yet. Or maybe, since he didn't have a car of his

own, he wouldn't be enough of a mechanic to know how
to do a job like that. Just the same I didn't do any
speeding on my way downtown.

I got myself a room at one of the smaller hotels where
I didn't know anybody and wouldn't have to do any
explaining, and put my car in the parking lot next door
to it. I got some magazines in the lobby and killed the
day reading and with a double feature movie. I didn't
run into anybody I knew.

After an early dinner, around six o'clock, it occurred
to me that possibly—contingent on what Joe Steiner did
after he'd heard what I had to tell him—it might be
advisable for me to stay at the hotel for several days
instead of only tonight. I'd been thinking of a one-night
stay when I'd tossed a few things into a bag and I'd need
a few things more. And this evening, right now, would
be the safest time for me to go home to get them.

I got the Buick out of the parking lot and drove home.

Almost home, anyway. As I turned the corner into my
block I saw a car parked facing the way I was heading,
across the street from my house and a few doors away
from it.

And the car was a jalopy, a black coupe, vintage of
about 1930. The jalopy that had followed me out of town
Friday afternoon.

If I'd had time to think I might have been afraid. But
there wasn't any time; if I was going to pull in and park
behind it instead of going past, I had to swing the wheel
right away. I swung the wheel and pulled in to the curb
behind the jalopy and only a few feet away.

•4•

The back window of the jalopy was small and not too clean; I still couldn't see who was behind the wheel. He must have been able to see back, though, well enough to recognize either me or the Buick. I heard the whir of his starter the moment I pulled to a stop behind him. But before he could get the engine going I was out of my car and alongside him.

Hard eyes looked at me from under carrot-colored hair. Pete Brenner, the Dead End kid best friend of Jimmy Chojnacki.

"Hello, Pete," I said.

He didn't answer. He tried to stare me down.

"Why did you follow me the other day, Pete? Why were you waiting here tonight?" I kept my voice calm. I just wanted to know; I didn't want to start trouble.

"You ought to know. Jimmy Chojnacki."

"What about Jimmy?"

"I got thinking after you and me talked. That accident didn't sound like one. I think maybe he was bumped off."

I said, "I think maybe you're a smart kid, Pete. I think Jimmy was bumped off too. Would you like to know who did it?"

"Are you kidding? He was my best friend."

I leaned a hand against the top of the car. "Good," I said. "Then we can get together on this. But when you got that idea, why didn't you just come to me? Instead of following me."

"Why should I trust you? I didn't know what your angle in it was."

"My angle? Hell, I showed you my press pass. I'm a reporter."

"But you're on vacation this week. I mean last week. You were on vacation the day you talked to me. I know that 'cause I *did* go down there to talk to you, after I got thinking about Jimmy, see? And then I got wondering about you too. What your angle was, if you wasn't working. And slipping me that fin—for nothing. That didn't add up either."

Yes, that had been a mistake, I saw now. I should have leveled with Pete Brenner and I'd have got more out of him—if he had anything to give me—than for any amount of money. Well, I had a chance to correct that now.

I said, "I see how it must have looked funny to you, Pete. But I was onto something big and I wanted to play it close to my vest. That's why I gave you the five, rather than explain."

"But what's this about vacation?"

"I gambled my vacation on getting a big story, that's all. Come on in the house with me. We can talk better there."

"We can talk all right here." I'd answered his questions but he was still suspicious.

"Sure," I said, "but we can talk better there. I think Jimmy was murdered. I think I know who killed him. But I'm not going to tell you standing here."

"All right." He got out of the car and followed me to the house, up on the porch.

I bent over and put the key in the lock. Something hard pressed into the small of my back. He said, "Stand still. I just want to see if you're heeled before I go in there with you."

I stood still and let him reach around me and feel for a shoulder holster, pat pockets. Then I turned the key and went in, snapped on the hall light. I looked around

carefully for any sign that I'd had a visitor again before
I said, "Let's go out in the kitchen. I'm going to have
a can of beer. Want one?"

"Sure."

When we were sitting at the table with a can of beer
apiece, I said, "Now listen, Pete, there's no reason why
I shouldn't tell you this—for practice, if for no other
reason. Tomorrow morning I'm going to be telling it to
the police, straight to Chief Steiner. But I want two
promises out of you before I start talking. One, you'll
keep this under your hat, talk about it to nobody. Okay?"

"Okay."

"The other, if I sell my idea to you, you won't try to
do anything about it on your own. No private revenge,
strictly up to the cops."

"Okay."

"It better be. Are you really carrying a gun?"

"Nah, that was a pipe I stuck in your back."

"All right, here we go. I think Obie Westphal killed
Jimmy."

He started to laugh and I waited till he finished. When
he quit laughing he stared at me. "What in hell gives
you a screwy idea like that?"

I told him, starting right at the beginning, the whole
story. Except that I left Oedipus in the closet and, of
course, I left Nina out of it. But I took the accidents at
the school one at a time, and told him about the freight
yards and—well, the whole works. Even and especially
what had happened last night.

"Jesus," he said when I finally stopped talking.

He believed me.

He said, "Jesus, I wish you'd told me this Wednesday.
It was me that damn near got you killed last night. I
talked to Obie about you yesterday afternoon, trying to
find out what he knew about you."

That was good hearing, although I couldn't tell him

so. It made me feel a lot better to know that Nina hadn't told Obie.

I said, "That wasn't your fault, Pete. Forget it. But now that you know the score, can you add anything? Was there anything you didn't tell me Wednesday that you can tell me now?"

He shook his head slowly. "No, damn it. But here's what happened with me. After you asked me them questions, I got thinking about what happened to Jimmy, and I began to think maybe he had been bumped off. I didn't have as much as you to go on; I didn't know about Obie's old man paying for the funeral or about Obie's leather being in Jimmy's pocket when he got killed. But I thought like you did about the racket that car makes going up the first hill on the roller coaster, and that Jimmy couldn't of not known the car was coming, see?"

I nodded.

"I did a lot of thinking that evening. Next morning I went in and quit my job—not just account of that, I'd been meaning to; it was a lousy job and I can get a better one. I wanted to talk to you and find out what your angle was, so I went down to the *Herald*. I know a copyboy works there. Billy Newman. So I ask him where to find you and he tells me you're on vacation, outa town fishing. That ain't the way I had it from you so I got curious about you. I made up my mind to watch you for a while and see what you were up to. Went out to your house early that evening. Your lights were on so I knew you weren't outa town like your paper thought."

"You followed me that evening?"

"Yeah, to the Press Bar somewhere around nine, came home about eleven, and went to bed. Anyway your lights went off and I went home. Didn't tell me much. I went back and tried again noon the next day. Tailed you downtown to a restaurant—I caught a sandwich across the street from it while you was eating—and then you started outa town on Seventy-one and I stuck with you. That's when you spotted me. Friday, that was.

"Well, after that I knew you'd know my car so I had to give that up. I did some more thinking and remembered you'd asked a question or two about Obie Westphal. So yesterday afternoon I looked him up and asked him if he knew you. He didn't and wanted to know what it was all about, so I told him about you asking questions about Jimmy Chojnacki and then about him, and that's how he got onto you."

"But what were you doing out front this evening?" I asked him. "You weren't going to try tailing me again in the same car, were you?"

"Nah, I'd decided to talk to you account I wasn't getting to first base. Waiting for you to get home. But when you pulled in behind me like that it scared me for a minute; that's why I'da scrammed if I coulda got the heap started quick enough. Say—"

"What, Pete?"

"You say the one night you tailed Obie he took a walk to the jungles. What time was it?"

"He left the house around nine, came back about half past ten."

"Maybe he'll go again tonight. And with two of us we maybe wouldn't lose him."

"Nix," I said. "I'm through. Tomorrow the police, and no more making like Nick Carter. Besides, don't you think he'll be *watching* for a tail tonight?"

"Sure, but he won't see one. We use my jalop'; he's never seen it. We park a long way off, just close enough to see his front gate. If he takes off for a stroll and heads toward the jungles we don't follow him, see? We take a different route and get there first. We'll be waiting back in the dark and pick him up after he comes in. And by that time he'll have watched for a tail all the way there and be sure he ain't got one so it'll be easy."

"Get thee behind me. No, Pete."

"Maybe you shouldn't, if he's ever seen you. Think he has?"

I thought back and said I didn't think so. He'd learned of my existence for the first time yesterday afternoon. I'd been playing poker at Harv Whelan's then and hadn't got home until midnight. Even if Obie had been watching the house and had seen me come home he would have seen me only at a distance and in the dark; I'd driven right into the garage and closed the doors from the inside. It had been plenty dark back there. I couldn't have been more than a shadow as I crossed from the side door of the garage to the back door of the house. And this morning I'd gone to the hotel early and had stayed downtown all day till an hour ago.

I said, "But he knows you, Pete."

"Don't worry about me. I can keep out of sight in a jungle." He stood up. "Well, I'm gonna try it anyway. If the cops pick him up after you talk to 'em tomorrow, this is my last chance not to miss out on all the fun."

"He probably won't go out tonight anyway."

Pete grinned. "Then what's to lose? I'll try it an hour or two anyway. So long."

I knew I couldn't stop him and I didn't want to let the fool kid go alone. I said, "Wait. Okay, I'll go along. We give up at ten o'clock." I looked at my watch. It was half past seven. "But give me ten minutes first. I came home to get a few things and I might as well while I'm here. Then we'll take both cars until we're a few blocks from Obie's; I'll leave mine there and get in yours. That way I won't have to come back here and you won't have to drive me downtown afterwards."

We did it that way. Pete parked the jalopy almost a full block away but at a point from which we could see the front fence and gate of the Westphal place. Far enough away that if he came out and walked toward us instead of toward the freight yards we'd have plenty of time to U-turn and get away. Or get down out of sight until he'd passed; the car itself wouldn't mean anything to him.

I hoped to hell that Obie would stay home and that nothing would happen.

At a quarter of nine Obie came through the gate and started walking the other way, toward the jungles.

We had plenty of time—it would take him twenty to twenty-five minutes to walk it and we could do it in five minutes in the car, even by a roundabout route so we wouldn't have to pass him—so Pete waited almost five minutes before starting the car. By then he'd be another block or two away and there wouldn't be a ghost of a chance of his hearing us take off.

Pete drove fast but skillfully. Half a block from the freight yards he turned the car into an alley and from the alley swung off onto the loading zone for a warehouse. We walked quickly back to the street and into the yards. In plenty of time; Obie wasn't yet in sight.

Not many strings of cars on this side of the yards tonight but two, on the fourth and fifth tracks over, were parallel and it was dark between them. The moon was bright but low in the sky; it was easy to see in the open but plenty dark in the shadows.

Looking through between two cars a few minutes later we saw him coming. He was walking into the yards at the same angle we'd taken. Pete said, "He's coming the way we did. He'll walk through here between these strings. Let's go down the line and find us an empty to duck in till he's past. Then we can follow him."

It sounded like good advice. We walked fast between the cars and the first empty was four cars down on our right. Pete climbed in. He said, "Come on. He'll be showing in a minute."

He was showing now, just walking around the end of the last car and starting toward us. Maybe I suddenly went a little crazy. I didn't get in after Pete. I whispered to him, "Get back out of sight and stay there. I want to talk to him. Stay right around the corner of the door so you can listen."

He whispered back, "Okay, pal," and then I couldn't see him any more.

If Obie could see me there in the shadows four cars away, it would be dimly. I had a little time to get ready. I whipped off my necktie and stuck it in my pocket. I turned the rim of my hat down all the way around and the collar of my coat up. I bent down and got a double handful of dust and rubbed it over the toes of my shoes. Then I brushed the worst of the dust off my hands and ran them over my face; luckily I hadn't shaved that morning and with dirt on top of a light beard it would look like several days' growth. Luckily too I'd been wearing this same suit most of the week without having it pressed, and it was a neutral color that didn't show whether it was clean or dirty. Even in the moonlight I could pass for a hobo.

I fumbled out a cigarette and stuck it in my mouth, then took a few steps to meet Obie as he came close. "Got a match, kid?" I asked him.

"Sure." He took a book of them from his pocket and lighted one for me and held it out in cupped hands. I held the tip of my cigarette to the flame.

His face, momentarily brightly lighted, grinned at me cheerfully. A schoolboy grin. So natural a grin that I couldn't help wondering if I was wrong down the line, if a series of coincidences had led me—

"Swell night, isn't it?" he said.

I nodded and just said, "Yeah," because my mind was doing handsprings trying to get back to believing what it had believed before. This kid couldn't be a killer. There was a catch somewhere.

"Just get in town?" he asked me.

I nodded. "How's work here?"

"All right, I guess. I'm still in school myself. What kind of work do you do?"

"Printer," I said. "Linotype operator. Say, do you—"

To the south of us a locomotive hooted and released steam and the clank of couplers drowned out what I'd started to say. The string of cars behind me was moving, and the car Pete Brenner was in was rolling away from us.

We both stepped back as the cars started to move. It put Obie's face in the moonlight. His eyes were boyishly eager. He said, "Let's hop 'em. I love to ride cars around the yards."

He ran lightly and grabbed the rungs of a car going by us. I hesitated; I almost didn't. If he'd urged me to do it, if he'd even looked around to see whether I was coming, I wouldn't have.

But he was climbing on up the rungs to the top of the car. The train wasn't going fast yet; it was easy for me to run and swing up after him. He was sitting on the catwalk when I got to the top. He was lighting himself a cigarette, again cupping his hands around the match.

He said, "Love to ride cars. Got to quit pretty soon though when school starts again. With studying and football I don't get time to come here. Ever play football?"

"No. Haven't the build for it," I said. Over the noise of the train and the rush of wind we had to talk loudly. I flipped my cigarette, a fiery arc into the night, and shifted to sit down more comfortably by the brake wheel. It was nice and cool up there. I didn't blame Obie for liking to do this.

I started to turn around to say something that would get him to talking again. My hand, resting lightly on the brake wheel, saved me from dying in the next second.

The push that sent me off the end of the freight car, into the space between it and the car ahead, was so sudden

and so strong that it would have knocked me off the car
even if I'd been ready and braced for it. But my left hand
tightened convulsively on the iron brake wheel and I
dangled there between the moving cars, only the narrow
coupling between me and the roadbed.

And Obie was bending over reaching for my fingers
to pry them loose from the wheel. Bending down that
way put his face in shadow; I still don't know whether,
in the act of murder, it was the smiling face of a schoolboy or the mask of a fiend. It's probably as well I didn't
see and don't know; I might be having nightmares about
it either way. I don't know which way would have seemed
the worse.

In that second of hanging on, of thinking I had only
another second or two to live, there was one part of my
mind that remained calm enough to cuss me out for the
utter fool I'd been. I'd *known*, and yet without even
thinking what I was doing I'd put myself in this spot.
I'd been so sure he wouldn't recognize me as Sam Evans
that I'd forgotten completely the fact that under these
circumstances I was in just as deadly danger whether he
knew me or not.

His hands were on my hand now, prying fingers loose.
I tried frantically to get my other hand up to the wheel
but I couldn't, with so precarious a grip, swing my body
to make my right hand reach that high.

Then, above and past Obie's head, I saw something
swinging down. Even over the noise of the train I heard
a thudding sound and then Obie was falling forward
toward me. My right hand managed to grab the edge of
the catwalk to supplement my failing grip on the wheel
and it pulled me in closer to the end of the car. Even
so, his body scraped against my back as he went over.

Then a hand grabbed my wrist to help me and it was
Pete Brenner, bending over the end of the car. Still in
his right hand was the pipe he'd had in his pocket. I

should have known; it wasn't a pipe for smoking. It was an eight-inch length of lead pipe.

He suddenly realized that he was still holding the pipe and that he didn't need it any more. He tossed it off the side of the car and used both hands to help me back up.

I looked down then. Obie was doubled over across the coupling between the cars but his body was starting to slide off. He went off head first; I saw his head hit the rail and then the car was over him.

A minute later the clank of couplings told us the train was slowing down, probably to reverse but we didn't wait for a ride back. We got off and took the quickest way out of the yards, and back along streets to where Pete had left his car.

We didn't talk much but Pete explained what had happened. When the car he was in had started moving, he'd stuck his head out of the door and had seen me following Obie up the rungs to the front end of the car that was three cars behind him. He'd jumped out of the door and caught the same set of rungs as it went by. He'd been holding onto them just below the top of the car, listening to us talk. Then when I'd yelled—I hadn't known that I had but it didn't surprise me—when Obie had pushed me, he'd come over the edge and slugged Obie while Obie was trying to pry my fingers loose from the wheel.

He drove me to my car and we parted there. I drove home and fast. I made a phone call to the airport and then phoned Millie. I told her everything was all right now and that not only could she come back but I desperately wanted her, needed her, to come back tonight, that if her brother-in-law would drive her to the airport right away she'd just make a plane that would get her home before midnight, and that I'd meet that plane. And she said that would be wonderful.

MONDAY

·1·

At nine-fifteen Harry Rowland went by my desk on his way out. He said, "Ed wants to see you, Sam." I got up and went into Ed's office.

He said, "How was the vacation, Joe?"

"Fine," I told him.

"I'll give you an easy one to start on. Funny thing, too. Remember the last day before your vacation we thought a kid named Westphal was the one killed at Whitewater and you were going to do a story on him?"

"I remember," I said.

"The Westphal kid *was* killed last night. Hopping cars in the freight yards, fell between 'em. Wheel went right over his head—but there's no doubt about identification this time."

"How much you want on it?"

"Don't spare the horses. His father's an advertiser, and Rowland says the kid was quite a high school celebrity in his own right. Rowland'll cover the details on the news end; you just write up the kid like you were going to do before."

"Sure," I said.

"Take your time and make it good."

I went back to my desk and fished in the back of the top drawer. It was still there, the story I'd written nine days ago. It began: "*Today under the wheels of a White-water Beach roller coaster—*" I took a thick soft copy pencil and obliterated that. I made it read. "*Last night under the wheels of a freight car at the C. D. & I. yards—*"

I read it through, all six pages, and didn't change another word. But I shouldn't turn it in for at least an hour, so I sat there staring at nothing. Until, up near the ceiling somewhere a fly started making a hell of a commotion. . . .

Also Available in Quill Mysterious Classics: